27

Wildfire!

LEFT BEHIND
>THE KIDS<

Jerry B. Jenkins

Tim LaHaye

WITH CHRIS FABRY

TYNDALE
KiDS

TYNDALE HOUSE PUBLISHERS, INC.
WHEATON, ILLINOIS

Visit Tyndale's exciting Web site at www.tyndale.com

Discover the latest Left Behind news at www.leftbehind.com

Published in association with the literary agency of Alive Communications, Inc., 7680 Goddard Street, Suite 200, Colorado Springs, CO 80920.

Edited by Curtis H. C. Lundgren

ISBN 0-8423-5791-2, mass paper

Printed in the United States of America

08 07 06 05 04 03
9   8   7   6   5   4   3   2   1

To Misty, Westin, and Brandi

TABLE OF CONTENTS

What's Gone On Before

JUDD Thompson Jr. and the rest of the Young Tribulation Force are in the middle of a great adventure. After an earthquake rocks Jerusalem, Judd and Lionel discover their friend Kasim has been killed. As they move through the rubble, they rescue the lead singer for The Four Horsemen, Z-Van. After Judd and Lionel help him to a doctor, Z-Van offers to fly them home.

Vicki Byrne and her friends, tucked safely away in a home in Wisconsin, watch prophecy being fulfilled as Nicolae Carpathia is assassinated in Jerusalem. The kids are disgusted by the outpouring of emotion for Carpathia and know that if Tsion Ben-Judah is right, Carpathia will soon rise from the dead.

Judd and Lionel try to tell Z-Van the truth, but the man won't listen. Instead of flying them home, Z-Van proceeds to New Babylon to honor the slain potentate.

Vicki is horrified to discover that her friend Charlie and the couple he was staying with are in GC custody. As Carpathia comes back to life, the kids realize the GC has traced Vicki's call to the Wisconsin hideout.

Amid killer lightning bolts, Lionel rushes back to their hotel. Judd moves closer to the stage to get a better look at the man he is sure is indwelt by Satan himself.

Join the Young Tribulation Force as they struggle to help their friends before another deadly prophecy comes true.

ONE

Into the Great Tribulation

JUDD Thompson Jr. wiped sweat from his forehead, aware that he was watching the beginning of the end of the world. For the past three and a half years he had studied biblical predictions about the Antichrist and the false prophet. There was no doubt in his mind that Nicolae Carpathia and Leon Fortunato, Carpathia's right-hand man, were the evil men described in Revelation 14 through 20.

The sun baked the crowd, still scurrying to greet the potentate. GC personnel in roving carts warned people that the courtyard was filled. "If you want to stay and watch the risen potentate greet others, feel free to do so. Otherwise, please exit the area. Thank you."

The gigantic screens showed Carpathia smiling, energetic, and full of life. Minutes earlier the crowd had wept over the man entombed in his glass coffin. Now, as the Bible had predicted, Carpathia stood in the midafternoon New Babylon sun and beamed. Like moths to a flame, the crowd worshiped their risen hero.

Judd felt drawn too, but for another reason. Carpathia's final words shocked him. The once-dead potentate had urged his enemies to join the Global Community. Then with menacing eyes the man spoke directly to believers in Christ and warned them not to attack him or the harmony he had worked hard to create. The look on Carpathia's face reminded Judd of the look on his face at the execution of the two prophets, Moishe and Eli. No doubt, Carpathia had the same in mind for other followers of Christ, but how would he try to kill them?

As Judd passed through the crowd, he overheard several people talking about Carpathia. "This is the greatest political comeback in history," a man said.

"There's nothing political about it," another said. "This is a religious experience! He's god!"

Judd shook his head as he headed for the courtyard. A GC guard with a bullhorn asked people to move away from the entrance.

Judd pulled out the special pass he had been given when he accompanied Z-Van backstage and held it high above his head. The guard didn't pay attention until Judd came closer. The man inspected the pass, eyed Judd warily, and motioned him through the gate.

"Why does he get to go through?" a woman yelled. "That's not fair."

The gate clanged shut and Judd moved past the line. He looped around the huge speakers and equipment at the front of the stage and found the narrow backstage stairs. He flashed his pass to another guard and the man waved him through.

Invited guests and dignitaries who had planned for a funeral watched in awe of Nicolae. Judd noticed some ashes behind the stage, the remains of the three regional potentates Leon Fortunato had struck with fire. Judd glanced at the statue of Nicolae, a perfect replica. Puffs of smoke lingered, and Judd shuddered as he recalled the voice that had thundered from it.

Judd walked through a series of curtains and almost tripped over Z-Van's wheelchair. A leg cast stuck out from under a velvet curtain. He pulled back the curtain and gasped when he saw Z-Van lying facedown, his hands raised in front of him. His guitarist, a skinny man known as Boomer, sat beside him, equally overcome.

Judd touched Z-Van's shoulder and the man turned, his eyes red. "Don't bother me. This is a holy moment."

"I can't take my eyes off Carpathia," Boomer whispered.

"Don't call him that," Z-Van snapped. "Don't even call him potentate anymore. The term is too low."

Z-Van took a quick breath and covered his face. "He's looking this way. I'm not worthy!"

Judd glanced up in time to catch Nicolae Carpathia staring straight at him.

Vicki's stomach churned as the kids scampered into the shadows of a rocky crag above Darrion's summer house in Wisconsin. The GC had located them through Vicki's phone call, but she could live with that. If she hadn't called her friend Natalie Bishop, they wouldn't have found out about the arrests of Charlie and the Shairtons.

Janie shook her head. "I liked this place. I thought we'd stay here a long time."

Mark cradled the laptop computer and

scanned their hideout below. "We have to figure a way out."

Two GC cars stopped near the driveway. Downed trees prevented them from driving all the way to the house. Radios crackled, then went silent as car doors opened and closed. Vicki couldn't see how many officers there were, but by the rustling of the leaves it had to be more than two.

"Be right back," Darrion whispered.

Vicki grabbed her arm. "What are you doing?"

"There's a path behind this rock that leads down to the driveway. I'm going to get a better look. Maybe I'll grab one of their radios."

Mark shook his head. "It's risky."

"I'll go with you," Vicki said.

Darrion squeezed between a tree and a rock, and the two wound around a tiny path. Vicki chose her footsteps carefully. In several places the path was so narrow that Vicki hugged the rock as she inched along.

"Don't look down," Darrion said.

Vicki glanced over the edge and saw tops of huge trees below. *No one could survive a fall that far*, she thought.

Darrion slipped on a loose rock and fell over the edge. She grabbed a small root and hung on as Vicki rushed to her. Rocks landed more than a hundred feet below.

Vicki grabbed Darrion's elbow and pulled with all her might. Darrion struggled to get a foothold and finally pulled herself up to safety. Vicki's heart raced like a frightened animal's as the two sat, their backs to the rock.

"Do you think they heard us?" Darrion panted.

Vicki gasped for air. "Let's go back to the others."

Darrion pointed. "Around this curve the cars will be directly below us. Come on."

Before Vicki could protest, Darrion was on the move. Vicki caught up, being careful not to slip. She leaned over the edge and spotted two GC cruisers near a thicket at the end of the driveway.

"Nobody's there," Darrion said. "Let's go."

"I thought you said the path leads down the hill."

Darrion smiled and pulled a rope from a hole in the rock and threw it over the edge. "My dad and I used to rappel down this rock face."

Darrion showed Vicki how to hold the rope and quickly slid down. When she reached the bottom, she waved.

Vicki took the rope like Darrion had shown her. She wasn't able to go as fast as

Darrion, and it felt good when her feet were on solid ground.

They ran to a tree and hid. From there they could see two GC officers outside the open front door of the house. One talked into a radio and gave orders. Darrion tugged at Vicki's shirt, and they crept toward the squad cars.

Darrion peeked inside an open window, grabbed a handheld radio from the passenger seat, and turned it on.

"Negative on the first floor," a man said. "Somebody's definitely been here, though."

One by one guards checked in with reports from inside the house. "This is quite a setup, sir. They've got a huge plasma TV and some pretty sophisticated equipment."

"This was Max Stahley's place," the leader said. "He liked the bells and whistles."

"If it was those kids, how would they have known about this place?" a female officer said.

"Good question."

"Let's go," Vicki whispered.

Darrion shook her head. "We have to think. Maybe we should let all the air out of their tires so they can't follow us."

Vicki glanced at the house again and made sure the officers hadn't moved. Darrion reached inside the car, pulled a lever, and the trunk opened with a thunk.

"What are you doing?"

"There might be stuff in there we can use."

"We don't need anything. Come on."

The leader barked orders to two guards outside. "We've got negative contact. Get the accelerant."

"What's that mean?" Vicki said.

Darrion hopped inside the trunk and pulled Vicki in with her.

Judd locked eyes with Carpathia and trembled. Could this man read Judd's thoughts? If Satan indwelt him, would he be able to see the mark of the believer on Judd's forehead?

Carpathia's face and body looked the same, but there was something different about his gaze. He seemed even more intense than before, as if some unearthly power surged through him. Nicolae turned and glanced at a woman in the receiving line. He smiled and spoke softly, reassuring her that he was alive and well.

Judd studied the back of Carpathia's head. There were no signs of the death wound inflicted by Dr. Chaim Rosenzweig at the closing night of the Jerusalem Gala. Judd relived the scene, remembering how Nicolae fell backward on Rosenzweig's razor-sharp sword. There should have been a huge scar on Nicolae's head, but hair had grown over it. Judd would have loved to inspect the wound closer, but he slipped behind a curtain out of Carpathia's sight. God's arch-enemy was only a few yards away, and the world worshiped him as if he were the creator of the universe.

Judd looked at Z-Van, still flat on the ground, groveling at the image of Carpathia. Judd heard Z-Van whisper something and he leaned closer.

"Victory to you, our lord and risen king, ruler of the world, head of everything," Z-Van said. "We bow and give you praise; once dead, you're now alive. May peace forever reign with you, our sovereign, Nicolae."

Judd closed his eyes and took a deep breath.

Z-Van turned and said, "If this doesn't make you a believer, nothing will."

Judd winced. He wanted to challenge Z-Van, tell him the truth again, but this wasn't the time or the place.

"Look at him," Z-Van continued. "He's got unbelievable power, even over death. When

I'm onstage and people scream my name and sing my words, it's an energy rush. But that's nothing compared to this." He looked at Nicolae again, his lower lip trembling. "This man is pure power, and I know he's back to help us."

Judd pulled the curtain back slightly and looked at the long line of people waiting their turn to greet Carpathia. He couldn't wait to get to Lionel and leave New Babylon.

Vicki scrambled inside the trunk, and Darrion pulled the lid down, making sure it didn't latch. A thin strip of light showed around the edge of the trunk lid.

"What if they're coming for this car?" Vicki whispered.

"Accelerant is like gasoline or something flammable. There are no cans in here."

"What will they do?"

"They're probably going to torch the house."

Footsteps hurried by and someone opened the other trunk, closed it, got in, and drove the car a few yards past them, gravel crunching under the tires. As Darrion started to lift the trunk to climb out, the officer in charge barked another order. "Move those fallen trees and bring the other car up here!"

"Told you we should have gone back," Vicki whispered.

As the GC guards groaned under the weight of the trees, Darrion fiddled with the trunk latch. "We'll wait until they start the fire and take off while they're not looking. But we've got to figure out a way to—"

Someone ran to the car and opened the driver's door. The car dipped to the left as someone sat. As the engine started, a warning buzzer sounded. The car sped toward the house and slid to a halt. Vicki thought she was going to fly through the backseat.

A man cursed as he slammed the front door. "Wonder who left this open?" The trunk lid slammed shut.

Mark Eisman scooted to the edge of the cliff and looked at the house. A GC officer handed two containers to the others, and the three went inside. Another car raced up, barely skidding to a stop before it smashed the other car. The man got out, slammed the trunk that was slightly open, and went inside.

Shelly crawled beside Mark. "Janie just came back. She said there's no sign of Vicki and Darrion."

Mark gritted his teeth. "We'll have to leave without them."

"No, I won't—"

Mark clamped a hand over Shelly's mouth. "Pretty soon they'll come looking for us and they won't be alone. We have to leave."

"But what if they're hurt? They could have fallen . . ."

"Let's find a safe place and regroup," Mark said. "Tell everybody we'll head along the trail Vicki and Darrion took. Maybe we'll find them back there."

As Shelly crawled away to alert the others, breaking glass shattered the morning stillness. Someone shouted and GC officers ran from the house.

Then Mark saw it. Smoke poured out of the windows of the Stahley home. Soon, flames licked at the walls. The GC officers were using their weapon of fire again. As the Stahley home went up in flames, Mark wondered what the GC's next weapon would be.

TWO

Wildfire

VICKI gasped, trying to catch her breath in the closed trunk. The heat and smoke quickly made it difficult to breathe. Darrion fiddled with the latch in the darkness, but it was no use.

"Don't use up all our air," Darrion snapped.

The radio Darrion still held crackled, and the GC leader ordered everyone away from the house. "Search the area thoroughly. I want those kids in custody!"

Someone jumped in the car and raced down the hill. Vicki's head hit the spare tire as she bumped into Darrion, the two rolling like luggage. The car screeched to a halt, and Vicki slammed against the backseat.

"This guy must have gotten his license off the Internet," Darrion said.

"We've found a vehicle," a female officer said moments later. "Illinois plates."

"Run them," the leader said.

"When they find out it's Bo and Ginny's car, the Shairtons will be in even more trouble," Vicki said.

Watching the flames shoot into the air, Mark gathered the others and found Darrion and Vicki's path. When they reached the dangling rope, Mark led them to the other side of the rock. Being careful not to make noise, they climbed behind a pine tree that seemed to grow straight out of the rock.

Squad cars screeched down the driveway, and Mark told everyone to get down. The two cars parked at the main road. "Looks like we're hiking out of here."

"What about Vicki and Darrion?" Shelly said.

"Maybe they've been caught," Janie said.

"We won't be able to help them if the GC catches us," Mark said. "Keep going."

The five headed up a small trail that led into the woods behind the Stahley home. Fire crackled in the distance. Conrad stopped them before they went over a ridge. "Those flames aren't just from the house. The fire's made it to the trees."

"Stupid," Mark said. "They're going to burn the whole forest."

Conrad picked up some brown pine needles and rubbed them between his fingers. The needles crackled and broke apart.

Janie pointed to a dry creek bed. "This place is going to blow like a firecracker."

"Which means firefighters will be here within a few hours," Conrad said. "We have to get out now."

Judd walked away from the stage, sure that he didn't want to be near Z-Van or the worship of Carpathia. He thought of Annie Christopher, the Global Community believer he had met who had been killed by Leon Fortunato's lightning. She had given her life trying to help others. Before she died, she talked about another GC worker who was a believer in Christ, but how would Judd ever find the man in this sea of humanity?

Most of the concession stands were abandoned or had sold out during the ceremony. Judd passed a first-aid station that looked like a mobile hospital. In addition to sunstroke and dehydration victims, doctors and nurses helped those who had been struck by lightning. But from the looks of the charred bodies, there wasn't much the medical staff could do.

Judd had been back in the sun only a few moments when he felt dizzy. He couldn't imagine what others who had been in the sun for hours were feeling. Such was their devotion to their risen leader. He found a strip of shade near another medical tent and sat. Huge monitors showed Nicolae and company still enjoying themselves. Carpathia, Fortunato, and a woman Judd didn't recognize shook hands, touched people's shoulders, smiled, and blessed each passerby.

Judd's shirt was wet with sweat and he was dying for water. A man peeked out of the tent. "We're tearing down. You have to move."

Judd nodded and walked toward the hotel. He had to get there before he passed out.

In Z-Van's hotel suite, Lionel Washington and Westin Jakes, Z-Van's pilot, watched the continuing coverage of Carpathia's triumphant return. Announcers were still dumbfounded at Nicolae's resurrection. Some commentators called him divine.

"What can you say about a guy who beat the odds like this," a man who had once been a sports commentator said. "With his back against the wall, two outs in the bottom of the ninth, Potentate Carpathia manages to cheat death out of its victory. Amazing!"

Reports from throughout the world showed an outpouring of emotion. People jammed the streets of London, Paris, and Moscow. In America, where the coverage of the funeral services had begun in the wee hours of the morning, people had gathered at sports stadiums to mourn together. When Carpathia came to life, they ran onto fields and courts and knelt before the giant screens.

One man in St. Louis had made a crude replica of Carpathia out of scrap metal. He placed the ten-foot-tall sculpture near the Mississippi River the night before the funeral. Thousands had knelt before the statue and prayed to Carpathia. Now the somber scene was replaced by people elated at the news of the potentate's rising.

Lionel thought of his friends in the States and wondered if Vicki and the others would come up with a new way to reach out with the truth. He logged on to the kids' Web site and read the latest postings.

Lionel explained to Westin about the Web site and Tsion Ben-Judah's writings.

Westin drank in every word. "I want to learn more. I don't want to waste any time."

"What do you mean?" Lionel said.

"I've spent the last few years flying Z-Van and his friends all over the world. Wild parties, booze, drugs, you name it. I've killed so many brain cells with those guys it's not funny, but now I'm walking away."

Lionel nodded. "I understand. When you know the truth, it's hard to be around people who don't. But you're in an important position."

"I don't follow."

"Z-Van trusts you. He'll listen to you. Even if he doesn't believe what you say about God, you might talk with his band members. Nobody has the access to important people and to travel that you do."

Westin sat on the bed and put his face in his hands. "I thought you'd tell me I needed to get away from these people as fast as I can."

Lionel sat beside him. "We have a couple of friends who had a chance to work directly for Carpathia. They both took the jobs, even though they were believers. They felt God wanted them in that place."

"I don't know," Westin said. "I want to help you and Judd get home, but—"

Westin's phone rang. He spoke softly for a few moments, then hung up. "That was Z-Van. I need to get him."

"I'll go with you."

When they were sure the GC guards couldn't hear them, Vicki and Darrion tore carpet from the trunk floor to get more air. The heat inside was amost unbearable. By prying the carpet from both taillights they got a little daylight, but they were still short of air.

"Do these backseats fold down?" Vicki said, kicking wildly.

"Don't," Darrion said. "We don't want to get caught."

"We're gonna smother if we don't get out of here!"

"See if we can find anything to help us get out," Darrion said.

Vicki found a crowbar and some roadside flares. Darrion pulled a fire extinguisher and a box from deep in the wheel well. As Darrion tried to open the box, the GC leader barked an order to bring the fire extinguishers from both cars.

"What do we do now?" Vicki whispered.

Darrion opened the box and found only some small tools. She pulled the pin on the fire extinguisher. "When they open the trunk, I'll spray them and we'll both run."

Vicki scooted to the rear so she could spring out. Someone ran past the car, opened the other trunk, and fumbled inside. The trunk closed and keys jangled. A key slid into the keyhole inches from Vicki's head, and she heard the man curse. He tried another key that didn't work. Something clunked on the ground, and Vicki assumed the man had dropped the fire extinguisher.

Before he could try again, the GC leader came back on the radio. "Forget about the extinguishers! The fire's getting away from us. Get out of here before the thing blows the other way."

Vicki sighed and sat back, not knowing whether to be thankful or upset. For the moment, while their air lasted, they were okay.

The GC guards jumped in and three doors slammed. The car turned around and sped toward the main road.

"What do we do with the car we found?" someone said on the radio.

"Leave it," the leader said. "The fire will take care of it and those kids."

As the car sped away, Vicki felt a rush of

air. She breathed deeply and gagged. Smoke wafted into the trunk.

Darrion leaned close. "Try not to cough. They'll hear us."

Mark started over the ridge but Conrad stopped him. Flames licked at the top of the rock. Gravel churned in the valley below as the two squad cars raced away.

"You still have the keys to the Suburban?" Conrad said.

"Yeah, why?"

"The GC are leaving. If the fire crosses the road, we could hike for a week and not find our way out of here."

Mark shook his head. "You think you can get it started?"

Conrad nodded. "It's our best chance."

Mark studied the hillside and handed the laptop to Shelly. "You, Melinda, and Janie head down the ridge and get to the road. Stay out of sight in case the GC come back."

"What are you going to do?" Melinda said.

"We're going to meet you at that curve in the road with Vicki and Darrion. Hurry."

Mark and Conrad raced down the embankment and found the trail. Smoke from the fire billowed into the air, and the smell was overpowering. Mark pulled his shirt over his nose and mouth.

The temperature rose as they got closer to the rope. Ashes and burning embers fell around them. Wind seemed to push the fire up the hill behind the house.

Conrad was first to the rope. He scampered down the rock easily, pushing off with his feet and sliding a few feet. A piece of burning ash fell on the rope and Mark stomped it out, but not before it burned a few strands. When he turned, Conrad was at the bottom, waving at him.

Mark pulled on the rope to make sure it would hold. His training with the militia had covered a lot about survival and being prepared, but his rock-climbing experience was limited to a wall back in middle school. He took a breath, tested the rope again, and started down.

"Throw me the keys," Conrad yelled from below.

Mark stopped, found the keys in his pocket, and let them fall. Conrad caught them and ran to the Suburban. Mark continued his descent one step at a time. He looked at the ground, felt dizzy, and decided it was best to look up. What he saw horrified him. A burning ember had fallen and the rope was on fire.

Mark hurried, trying to imitate Conrad's rapid movements, but he couldn't go as fast. When he was twenty feet from the ground, the rope frayed then snapped, and Mark screamed all the way to the ground. He felt the air whoosh out of him, and for a few moments he couldn't talk, couldn't breathe. Conrad helped him up and Mark pointed to the car.

"Just get it started," Mark gasped.

When Mark arrived, Conrad had the hood up and was spraying something near the engine. "Bo said this might help if the car wouldn't start. I forgot about it until now."

Mark looked at the Stahleys' house, completely engulfed in flames. He yelled for Vicki and Darrion but no one answered. Several explosions rocked the hillside, and Mark wondered what kinds of explosives Mr. Stahley had hidden inside. The flames had spread to the trees behind the house and were working their way around the ridge. A huge plume of white smoke hung over the valley.

Mark climbed a knoll and looked at their way of escape. The wind had swirled the fire toward the road a few hundred yards ahead. He ran back to Conrad. "Get that thing started now!"

"I'm doing the best I can," Conrad said, capping the spray can and climbing into the driver's seat. The engine turned over a few times but wouldn't start.

"We'll have to make a run for it," Mark said.

"What about Vicki and Darrion?"

"Either the GC got them or they're on foot. Let's go."

"Give me one more chance," Conrad said.

As the fire ate more trees, the heat grew unbearable. Mark turned his back to it and covered his face and arms.

Conrad opened something near the engine, sprayed furiously, then slammed the hood and hopped back into the front seat. "God, we need your help." He turned the key and the engine sputtered, then chugged faster and faster until it sparked to life. Conrad floored the gas and the engine revved wildly.

"Woo-hoo, we're in business!" Mark yelled.

Mark pushed the car out of the bushes. He dived into the passenger side as Conrad pulled away. As they rounded the first curve, Conrad slammed on the brakes. The road ahead was a wall of fire.

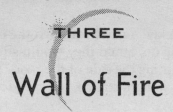

THREE

Wall of Fire

MARK looked behind them and saw the road ended just past the Stahley home. "We'll have to hoof it."

Conrad shook his head. "If we get up enough speed, we can go right through it."

"Won't the gas tank explode in the heat?"

"This thing is built like a tank. Let's give it a shot."

Mark thought of his cousin, John, who had spent his last moments on earth watching a fiery meteor slam into the Atlantic Ocean. "What if the tires start to melt?"

"Trust me. If we get enough momentum, we'll be fine." Conrad slammed the car in reverse and backed around the curve. He threw the Suburban into gear and mashed the accelerator to the floor.

The car was sluggish at first but picked up

speed quickly. As they rounded the curve, Mark hung on, afraid they would slide into the trees lining the side of the road. When they hit a straight stretch, the speedometer went crazy.

"How wide do you think the fire line is?" Conrad yelled over the engine noise.

Mark swung his seat belt around his shoulder and clicked it. "Wide enough to cook us if we stop."

"Hang on!" Conrad yelled.

As the GC car sped along the rural road away from the fire, Vicki prayed for her friends. Someone in the other car radioed the leader. Darrion kept the volume down and held it so she and Vicki could hear.

"I want you away from that fire," the leader said, "but set up a lookout just before the main road. If those kids are back there and the fire doesn't get them, that's where they'll probably come out."

Darrion shook her head. "I have to get more air." She wedged the crowbar into the trunk lid.

Vicki saw a little daylight, but some black strips of rubber blocked it. She helped pull at the rubber, and Darrion bent the trunk enough to let in a little more air.

The men in front talked, but the droning of the car's tires made it impossible to hear them. The radio crackled again, and the leader identified himself to the base in Des Plaines. He asked to be patched into GC Wisconsin Emergency Management. Moments later a deep-voiced man asked about the situation.

"Two things," the leader said. "We've got a wildfire in some dense woods north of Lake Geneva. You're going to need a big crew to fight this one."

"We just got a report about that from a civilian," Deep Voice said.

The leader gave them the exact coordinates of the fire. "The other situation is a group of kids who might be on foot. We think they started the fire."

"What?" Vicki said in a hoarse whisper.

Darrion put a finger to her lips.

"You talking rescue?" Deep Voice said.

"Not exactly. We think one is the girl who jammed the GC satellite school uplink."

"I heard about that. Why don't you stay and take care of them?"

"We're leaving one squad near a main road in case they come that way. I need to get back

to Des Plaines to interrogate our prisoners.
Found some interesting information up here."

"He's going to make the Shairtons pay for
giving us the truck," Vicki said.

"We'll keep you informed if we see
anything," Deep Voice said. "Chopper's
headed that way, and they've scrambled an
emergency fire crew."

Judd knew he had been in the sun too long.
His lips were chapped and his legs felt numb.
Sweat dripped from his face as he moved
through the crowd, trying to remember the
way back to the hotel. The main stage was a
few hundred yards away. He thought the
hotel was to his left, but he wasn't sure.

Judd turned and squinted, shimmering
vapors rising from the asphalt in the
distance. His head felt light and he closed his
eyes for a moment. He needed something to
lean against.

A speaker stood a few yards away and Judd
lurched forward, hoping his momentum
would carry him. He needed to collect his
thoughts and find some water.

A group of ten passed nearby and a teenager ran up to them, out of breath. "Any
luck?" an older man said.

"You won't believe it," the boy said. "I was just at the palace. We were told the potentate cannot see any more visitors than the ones in line."

"Tell us something we don't know," a woman said.

"But a man shouted an idea to one of the guards," the boy continued. "He asked if we could worship the statue! It will be more than an hour before we're allowed in, but they have given the okay."

The group cheered and rushed to get in line, and Judd followed. Suddenly, he heard the high-pitched drone of a small engine and someone behind him shouted, "Look out!" Judd turned to see a man in a golf cart bearing down on him.

He couldn't move. Judd had heard about animals being caught in the headlights of an oncoming car, unable to budge from their spot in the road. Now Judd knew exactly how they felt. The man in the cart slammed on his brakes and slid. At the last second, Judd closed his eyes and prepared for the impact.

Something pushed him and he had the sensation of flying, moving through the air effortlessly.

Then everything went black.

Moments before they hit the wall of flame, Mark had second thoughts. He wanted Conrad to stop, but they were flying now, doing more than eighty miles per hour on a road that didn't even have a posted speed limit. Even with their windows rolled up, Mark felt the fire's heat as they raced toward the orange flames. A burning tree began to fall and Mark pointed at it. Conrad kept going as the tree fell behind them.

The car was inside the inferno only a few seconds, but it felt like an hour. The speed of the Suburban carried them through the firestorm. When they came out on the other side, Conrad and Mark whooped and hollered. Conrad jammed on the brakes and they stopped a few feet short of an embankment.

Mark jumped out to inspect the car. The fire had left black spots on the peeling paint. Conrad sprayed windshield-wiper fluid and steam rose from the glass.

A smoky cloud rose above them as the fire devoured everything in its path. It was moving more quickly now, blowing along the road and up both sides of the hill.

Mark jumped back inside and Conrad rushed along the road, keeping an eye out for the others. Mark looked at the mountain engulfed in flames and smoke. *This fire is just like the Global Community,* he thought. *It ruins everything it touches.*

"We're coming to the curve you showed the girls," Conrad said.

Mark asked him to slow down and the two kept watch for any movement. A rock banged off the roof and Conrad stopped. Shelly, Melinda, and Janie climbed over the road's edge and got in the car.

"What took you so long?" Janie said.

"Had a little problem getting it started," Conrad said.

Shelly looked around inside. "Where are Vicki and Darrion?"

Mark explained what they had found.

"You think they could have been in one of the GC cars?" Melinda said.

Mark shook his head and took the laptop from Shelly. He had no idea where Vicki and Darrion were or if they were still alive.

Lionel was amazed at the number of people in the street, singing, dancing, and chanting about Carpathia, their new god. Several people banged on the side of their vehicle, asking for a ride to get closer to Carpathia.

Westin told Lionel not to roll down the windows, and the people finally backed away, clearly upset.

They made it through the crowd and the gauntlet of GC security poised near the courtyard. Lionel walked behind Westin as they approached the stage where Carpathia, smiling, still greeted people. It seemed like every third person fainted as they prepared to shake Carpathia's hand.

As Westin went for Z-Van, Lionel studied the monitor behind the stage and listened closely as Carpathia soothed each person with his voice. He must have said "Bless you" a hundred times while Lionel watched.

What shocked Lionel most was hearing Leon Fortunato speak to all the people as they passed. "Worship your king," he said. "Bow before his majesty. Worship the Lord Nicolae, your god."

Guards in the background tried to move people along, but Carpathia and Fortunato didn't seem concerned about the thousands still waiting in line. They drank in the praise together.

Lionel looked over the audience, hoping to spot Judd. The sector Lionel had left him in was deserted. Candy wrappers and drink cups littered the ground, but there was no breeze, just the hot sun beating down on the asphalt. *He's probably back at the hotel watching this on TV*, Lionel thought.

Westin wheeled Z-Van to the stairs. The singer beamed and mumbled something as they carried him to the van. Lionel leaned close and heard Z-Van say, "The face of god. I've seen the face of god."

Throughout the ride to the hotel, Z-Van rambled on about Carpathia and his powers, Leon Fortunato's lightning show, and the crowds. Lionel listened but didn't talk. Finally Z-Van looked at him and said, "I saw your friend earlier. Where is he?"

"I'm hoping Judd's at the hotel. We got separated after Carpathia—I mean, Potentate Carpathia came alive."

Z-Van stared out the tinted window. "Nobody's ever experienced what we did today. I know you guys believe Jesus came alive, but that was in some cave in Israel, and nobody saw it happen. This was live, in front of cameras and millions of people. His Excellency doesn't do anything in secret."

Lionel sighed. He wanted to ask Z-Van about Judd but he held his tongue.

Westin spoke up. "What's up next on the schedule?"

Z-Van stared straight ahead. "He looked at

me—he spoke with his eyes. He said he had heard the song, even though he was dead."

"You mean Carpathia?" Westin said.

"He spoke to my heart." Z-Van suddenly sat up. "That's it! I'll make a monument to him, just like the one they had in the courtyard, only this one will be music dedicated to Lord Carpathia."

Lord Carpathia? Lionel thought.

"Cancel everything and get the band together," Z-Van continued. "I want no interruptions."

"What about Judd and Lionel?" Westin said.

"Who?"

"The kids who saved your life," Westin said, pointing to Lionel. "You told them you'd give them a ride back to the States."

Z-Van shook his head. "They'll have to wait."

As Conrad drove toward the main road, Mark turned on the computer and checked the Web site for any e-mail. He found a message from Natalie, who had been reassigned to GC headquarters in Des Plaines.

Good news, Natalie wrote. *The adult Tribulation Force made it out alive. No one was taken into custody. I don't know how they did it, but the GC around here are pretty upset.*

Also heard a report that you guys set a fire up there. Please let me know your situation as soon as possible.

"She didn't say anything about Vicki and Darrion being taken into custody," Mark said.

"They can't be in the woods," Conrad said. "We yelled at the top of our lungs."

The road wound around a hill and angled down. Dust rose behind them. Shelly pointed ahead. "There's the main road."

Conrad picked up speed and skidded sideways onto the pavement. Mark looked back to see a perfect view of the mountain, dense smoke rising above it.

Something moved from behind a row of bushes near the road, and Janie screamed. "It's a GC squad car!"

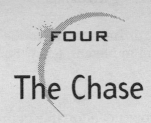

FOUR

The Chase

MARK watched the GC car speed up. It was newer, faster, and would overtake them quickly.

"Floor it!" Mark said.

"I am," Conrad said, watching the speedometer slowly climb.

"They're gaining on us!" Shelly said.

"Is there anything in the back we can throw out to slow them down?" Mark yelled.

Shelly and Janie climbed over the backseat. "There's a spare tire and a tire iron," Shelly said.

"I found a bunch of nails and screws in a little box," Janie yelled.

Mark turned to Conrad. "Go as fast as you can. We'll slow them up a little."

Conrad nodded and kept his eyes on the road as Mark climbed over the seats. He grabbed the tire iron, smashed the back window, and muttered, "Sorry, Bo."

Vicki tried to get comfortable in the trunk. Darrion held the crowbar in place so they would continue to get air.

"Where do you think they're going?" Darrion whispered.

"Probably back to Des Plaines where they're holding the Shairtons and Charlie."

A frantic voice came on the radio, calling the leader. Vicki's heart sank as she heard a young officer say, "We've got those kids, sir. They're in that old car we spotted in the bushes. They're about a quarter of a mile ahead of us."

"How many?"

"Can't tell, sir. They passed us going pretty fast. Probably at least four or five."

"Where are they headed?"

"Toward Lake Geneva, sir."

"Good," the leader said. "The roads are torn up that way. You should be able to catch them."

"We'll need some backup to transport that many, sir."

"Right. I'll arrange it. Just catch them!"

"Sir, they're—whoa!" the young officer said. His radio went dead.

"What's wrong?"

"Sir, they're throwing things from the back of the car. We had to swerve around some debris of some sort—watch out!"

The radio went dead again, and then the young officer came back on, breathless. "They just threw a tire out. We're trying to get back on the road."

"Stay a safe distance behind," the leader shouted. "Just keep them in sight until we can get the chopper headed your way."

Judd's first thought was of heaven. Have I died? He moved his head back on the pillow and struggled to open his eyes. When pain shot through his body, he knew he wasn't in heaven. He yelped and settled back on the pillow.

He felt a bandage on his left arm and noticed his legs were wrapped tightly with gauze. Red spots showed at his elbow, and his shirt was torn and bloody. A bag of fluid hung beside his bed, and there was a needle in his left hand. Every breath was like swallowing shards of glass through this crack down his parched throat.

Cots filled the room as emergency medical personnel hurried about. The tent flap opened, and two GC officers with huge sweat stains showing through their uniforms carried a body inside.

"Not in here," a woman said. "Next tent."

"Sorry, ma'am," the officer said.

Judd lifted his head slightly and studied the patient next to him. The man's face was as red as a cooked lobster. On the other side of Judd was a woman lying on her side, her back to him. She had long, brown hair and her knees were drawn to her chest.

When a nurse approached, Judd tried to talk. The woman shook her head and put a finger to her lips. "I'll be with you in a moment."

The nurse knelt by the cot of the brown-haired woman. When the patient didn't respond to her questions, the nurse felt for a pulse, then turned the woman on her back. To Judd's horror, a black mark ran down the side of the woman's neck. The nurse quietly covered the woman's body and moved to Judd.

"Water," Judd managed.

The woman asked someone to bring a bottle. She knelt by Judd, felt his forehead, and checked his bandages. "You gave us a scare."

"What happened?" Judd said.

"The man who brought you in said you stepped in front of his cart. He slammed on his brakes, but the impact knocked you down and you fell on the pavement." She pulled the bandage back from his arm and winced. "Fortunately, you didn't land on your head. They said the asphalt is one hundred and twenty degrees in the sun."

Judd tried to sit up, but his head became light and he felt sick to his stomach.

"You've lost a lot of fluid," the nurse said, checking the IV. "We need you strong so you can join in the worship of the risen potentate."

"I need to get to my—"

"Lie still," the nurse said, pushing Judd back on the cot.

Judd glanced at the dead woman. "What happened to her?"

"Lightning," the nurse said. "There were many who ran when the supreme commander told them not to. It's a shame. Maybe this is a way to weed out those weak in faith."

Judd closed his eyes and wanted to scream. Some of those who had been struck were believers in the true God. Others had apparently been scared of a dead man coming back to life.

The nurse gave Judd a bottle of water with a straw. He grabbed her hand as she turned to leave. "I need to get a message to my friend."

She pulled a pencil and a scrap of paper from her pocket. "Write it down and I'll be back later to check on you."

"But—"

"People are dying. I have to go."

Judd turned on his side and tried to write but his eyes stung. Whatever the doctor had given him for the pain was wearing off. The scrapes on his arms and legs burned like fire. The smell of the dead turned his stomach and he thought he would be sick. Finally, he turned over on his cot, buried his head in the pillow, and fell asleep.

Lionel wondered about Judd as he stared at the locked door to Z-Van's room and listened to the clanging of the man's guitar. Glass smashed and Z-Van cursed.

Boomer, Z-Van's lead guitarist, lit a cigarette and slid down the wall to the floor. "He always gets like this when he's in one of his creative moods. You can bet this is going to be a good album if he's working this hard."

Lionel pulled Westin into another room.

"I'm worried about Judd. I need to know what he said to Z-Van backstage."

"You don't know what you're asking," Westin said.

"That guy could have turned Judd in for all we know. He could be in GC custody. I want to find him and get out of here before Z-Van goes berserk."

"You're this scared of him and you want me to stay and work for him?"

Lionel sighed. "I don't know what you should do, but I can't wait any longer. It'll be dark soon. Please."

Westin knocked on Z-Van's door, and the man flew into a rage. A mirror shattered and something hit the wall and broke. Finally, Z-Van opened the door and Westin slipped inside. Z-Van screamed, a lightbulb shattered with a pop against the door, and Westin yelled back.

As the noise increased, Boomer stood, stretched, and said he was going to rest in another bedroom. A few minutes later Westin returned, holding a cold soda can on a red welt above his eye. "That went well." Westin smirked.

"Did he tell you about Judd?"

"Just about the song he was composing when Judd interrupted his worship of

Carpathia. He said Judd looked a little sunburned, but he didn't remember him saying much."

"You don't think Z-Van turned him in?"

"I don't think Z-Van has thought two seconds about anything but Carpathia. He's bought the lie big time."

Lionel grabbed a bottle of water and opened the front door. "I'll call in an hour. If Judd comes back, tell him to stay put."

Mark threw everything he could get his hands on out the back, hoping to slow down the GC car. They had swerved at each load he threw, but the car kept coming.

"I see the lake," Conrad shouted from the front.

Mark turned and saw water to their right. The road wound around the lake and into town, a couple of miles away.

"Where should we go?" Conrad said.

"Head for town," Mark said. "We've got a better chance of losing them there."

Conrad sped up. Janie handed Mark an ashtray and the rest of the food. "Only thing left is the laptop."

"What about the seats?" Shelly said.

"Good idea," Mark said. "Help me unhook

them. Janie, see if you can get the back door open."

Mark, Shelly, and Melinda worked furiously to unlatch the two bench seats. They pushed and pulled the seats to the open door in back.

"Don't fall out!" Conrad called out, looking in the rearview mirror.

The GC car had gained ground and followed only a few car lengths behind. Janie held the door open as Mark and Shelly prepared to launch the smaller bench.

"The guy has a gun!" Janie said.

Mark heard the first ping of a bullet glance off the fender. "They're trying to shoot out our tires!"

"The town's coming up," Conrad yelled. "There's a bridge ahead."

"I don't remember a bridge around here," Mark said.

"Maybe they built it after the earthquake," Conrad said.

Another bullet pinged, and the kids threw themselves behind the seats, the back door swinging wildly.

"When I say, we push both of these out at the same time," Mark shouted.

An explosion rocked the car and the Suburban careened out of control, almost hitting the guardrails on the bridge. Mark smelled rubber burning as one of the back tires shredded. The Suburban slowed as the GC car swerved onto the bridge. "Get ready!"

The GC car wasn't far behind when the kids shoved the seats out. They landed on top of each other, skittering on the pavement in opposite directions. The car turned and avoided the smaller seat, but it hit the larger one full force, pinning it under the front tires. The car skidded to a stop.

It was dark as Lionel walked toward the palace, thousands of people filling the streets, celebrating, drinking, and dancing. Loud music blared from speakers hastily set up outside restaurants and hotels. Anyone who passed by was drawn into the celebration.

A young woman grabbed Lionel and pulled him into a crowd screaming Carpathia's praises. She took his arms, danced in a circle, and shouted, "He is risen!"

Lionel smiled, but the woman jerked on his arms. "Come on, say it!"

"He is risen," Lionel muttered.

"No, you're supposed to say, 'He is risen indeed.' "

"Yeah, right. He is risen indeed."

The woman danced again, hopping and skipping, running into others in the crowd as she circled with Lionel. "He is risen," she shouted again.

"He is risen indeed!" a man said, pushing Lionel away and moving toward the woman.

Lionel slipped out of the crowd, glad to be away from the revelers. He shuddered as he walked toward the palace. Early Christians had used those same words about Jesus. *Is there anything followers of Carpathia won't do?*

Mark led the cheers as the kids screamed. He fell to the floor and kicked his feet high in the air as the GC officers got out and tried to dislodge the seat.

"There's no time to celebrate," Conrad yelled. "We can't go any farther on this bad wheel."

Mark tried to close the back door, but it was stuck. The shredded tire was almost gone, and the wheel made a *ka-thunk* sound each time it went around. The metal rim was surely bent.

A louder thumping beat the air outside the car. Mark glanced out the back and saw a helicopter swoop low behind them.

"We've got more company!" Mark shouted. "Go faster!"

"I've got it to the floor," Conrad said. "We have to ditch this thing."

Smoke rose from the shattered tire. Mark knew it could catch on fire, and if the sparks reached the gas tank, they'd be blown sky-high.

Shelly put a hand on Mark's arm. "What now?"

FIVE

Chased by the Dragon

MARK crawled to the front of the car as Conrad turned down a tree-lined street. A brick building stood to the right and the lake lay beyond it. The helicopter hovered overhead.

"Can you get us to the main street?" Mark yelled.

"No way!" Conrad said. "Get in the back. I'll tell you when to jump."

Mark wanted to argue, but he knew Conrad was right. They had to get out now. Mark gathered the others at the rear.

"What about Conrad?" Shelly said.

"He'll get out. Just be ready."

"I don't like this," Janie said.

Mark cradled the laptop in his arms. He hoped to time his jump and protect the computer.

Conrad drove off the pavement and onto a small knoll under an oak tree. "Now!"

Janie, Melinda, and Shelly jumped out and rolled on the grass, the car still moving. Mark jumped, landed on his feet, and rolled backward, narrowly missing a fire hydrant. He patted the laptop and turned to watch the Suburban.

The car accelerated over the knoll, and Mark lost sight of it for a moment. It raced up an embankment that led to a short pier, careened off the edge, and landed in the water.

"Come on!" Mark shouted. He and the others raced to the brick building and watched the Suburban sink into the muddy lake.

Shelly put a hand over her mouth. "We have to help Conrad!"

The GC helicopter passed overhead and hovered over the choppy water. The car lay on its side, sinking quickly. Mark noticed several people on the sidewalk near the main pier, watching the scene.

Shelly started toward the lake and Mark grabbed her arm. "He wouldn't want you to put yourself in danger!"

Shelly pulled away, put her head on Melinda's shoulder, and cried.

"Look!" Janie said.

Conrad scampered up the hill in the cover of some shrubs. "What's all the blubbering about?"

Mark socked him in the shoulder and Shelly hugged him. Conrad caught his breath and said, "I wedged my shoe onto the accelerator and jumped out just over the hill. I don't think the GC saw me."

Mark looked toward the road leading to town. It was their only hope. The kids ran away from the brick building and crossed the street, making sure they kept trees between them and the helicopter. They passed a long building with a screened-in area, and Mark remembered it had once been a seafood restaurant.

People from the town crowded near the pier, pointing and asking questions. A teenage boy in cutoff jeans said he had seen the whole thing. "That truck passed the library and headed straight for the water. I don't think anybody could have survived a crash like that."

An older woman shielded her eyes. "How many were in it?"

"I don't know. The driver was probably drunk."

The kids turned left and ran up another street. Before the disappearances the town had been a vacation spot for Chicago area families. Now shops that once sold ice cream and T-shirts were boarded up.

The helicopter moved from its position over the water, apparently convinced that the kids weren't in it or hadn't survived. Mark pulled the others into a doorway until the chopper passed. A siren wailed in the distance.

"Come on," Mark said.

The kids ran farther up the street, passing more boarded-up businesses. Mark darted into an alley and the others followed.

Conrad grabbed Mark's arm. "I think we can get in this building."

Conrad pried two boards from a rickety door that led to one of the abandoned shops. The doorknob fell off, Conrad kicked, and the door flew open. Once inside, Conrad replaced the boards.

Mark and the others moved through a narrow hallway to the front of the store and were surprised to find it had once been a bookstore. Shelves lined the walls, and there were still a few books in piles on the floor. A large window in the front gave them a view of the street and part of the lake.

Mark pulled out his wallet, checked his cash, and made a face.

"What is it?" Melinda said.

"The cash box. Did anybody remember it?"

Conrad groaned. "It must still be in the glove compartment."

The kids went through their pockets but came up with only a few Nicks. Because no one had eaten since the day before, they pooled their money, and Shelly volunteered to find some food.

"I don't think we should go out before dark," Conrad said.

"I'm starving," Janie said.

"I won't go far," Shelly said. "If I see any GC, I'll come right back."

Mark paced the floor as Shelly climbed out the back. A few minutes later a GC car passed and the kids hit the floor. The car's engine sounded funny, and Mark peeked through a hole in the boarded-up window. "It's the GC car that followed us."

"How can you tell?" Janie said.

"Front end's out of whack," Mark said. "Must have taken a while to get that seat out."

The GC turned on the car's loudspeaker. "Citizens of Lake Geneva, we need your help locating some enemies of the Global Community and the risen potentate. We believe they are between the ages of fifteen and twenty. If you see anyone you do not know, please report them immediately to this squad car or the GC post set up at the pier."

Shelly returned and Conrad helped her inside. She placed a paper bag on the floor and pulled out a loaf of bread, some bologna and cheese, and a few bottles of water. "I would have bought more, but I ran out of money."

Shelly explained that she had found a gas station a few blocks away that had a few high-priced supplies. She hadn't heard the GC loudspeaker.

"We'll lay low until dark and try to make a break," Mark said.

Lionel moved in the darkness toward the courtyard. Pilgrims had formed a new line in front of the giant statue of Nicolae. As they passed it, some reached out and touched the legs of the image. Others knelt, bowed, or lay prostrate before it, praying and worshiping the idol.

Lionel's mind raced thinking about all the things that might have happened to Judd. He could have been arrested by the GC, or worse, he could have been struck by Leon Fortunato's lightning.

Many of the medical tents were empty. Others bustled with activity as medical personnel tried to care for the injured and those suffering from the heat. He stumbled into one tent that was eerily quiet and smelled like smoke. A guard approached.

"I'm looking for a friend of mine."

The guard said something in a different language. When Lionel shook his head, the man said, "Dead here. You look for lightning dead?"

"No. I mean, I don't know."

The man pointed to a tent a few hundred yards away, and Lionel thanked him. A nurse approached Lionel in the next tent, and he explained what Judd looked like. The woman shook her head. "I haven't seen anyone who fits that description, but I've only been here an hour."

"Can't you look up his name?"

"We've been treating people as they come in. We don't have a database yet. Look around, but don't bother anyone and don't get in our way."

Lionel tiptoed through the rows of cots, looking into faces of strangers. Most were asleep, trying to overcome the effects of the hot day. Others moaned.

One man reached out to Lionel as he passed. "Something for the pain!"

"I can't help you."

The man grabbed Lionel's shirt, but Lionel pulled away.

Other patients stirred and a nurse ushered Lionel outside. He tried to explain, but the woman wouldn't listen. "Don't let him back inside," the woman said to a guard.

Judd saw his friends running away and he shouted, but they kept running. One of them fell and turned toward him. It was Nada. Judd called out as someone helped her up, and he realized it was his old friend Ryan Daley. A dog barked. Judd turned and saw a hideous dragon, eyes red and tongue full of fire.

Someone grabbed Judd and pulled him toward the others. It was Annie Christopher, the GC employee he had met at Carpathia's funeral.

Judd's legs were heavy. He tried to run, but he felt the hot breath of the dragon behind him. He glanced back and screamed as the dragon came close, its breath horrible, fangs bared, ready to strike.

Judd sat up in bed, out of breath. The dream had been so real he was shaking. He looked for a nurse and saw one at the front of the tent, ushering someone outside. He blinked and tried to focus. Could it be?

"Lionel!" Judd said weakly.

Judd ripped the needle from the back of his hand and jumped to the floor. His legs gave way and he fell, catching himself on the side of the next cot. He wasn't going to let his friend leave without him.

Vicki tried to stay awake as the car drove on. She didn't want to be overcome by any fumes, so she stayed close to the opening Darrion had made, breathing in the clean air.

Throughout the trip, Vicki heard radio reports about the kids in Wisconsin and the wildfire that was completely out of control. One guard contacted the other car and asked if they had seen his radio. Darrion stifled a laugh.

When someone reported that the Suburban had plunged into Lake Geneva, Vicki's heart sank. A few minutes later the chopper pilot said no one had come to the surface.

"If they're not dead, they're on foot," the leader said.

"Search the town. I want those kids brought in for questioning, especially the one that interrupted the satellite feed."

Darrion smiled at Vicki. "What's it feel like to be a wanted teenager?"

Vicki rolled her eyes. "Really special."

The GC stopped and Darrion took the crowbar from the trunk. One officer got out and returned with drinks for the others. Vicki realized how thirsty and hungry she was.

An hour later a report from the emergency management team informed the officers that the wildfire was gaining on the town of Lake Geneva. "We're digging a fire line to see if we can contain it. It's already destroyed a number of homes. It'll be a miracle if we can stop it before it gets to town."

"I can't believe they're blaming us for the fire," Darrion said.

"Typical."

The next time they stopped, all the officers got out and Vicki heard other car doors slam nearby. Darrion put the crowbar under the trunk lid and lifted an inch or two. They were at a police station.

"You think this is where they're holding Charlie and the Shairtons?" Darrion said.

Vicki smiled. "Wasn't it nice of them to give us a ride?"

Darrion tried to use the crowbar to break the latch. When she couldn't, she started to bang and Vicki touched her shoulder. "Somebody might hear us."

Vicki concentrated on the backseat. She pulled the covering material away and kicked as hard as she could. The seat gave a little.

"There must be some kind of latch up front that pops the thing forward," Darrion said.

Vicki felt along the top of the seat but couldn't find a button or a latch. "Let me try," Darrion said.

Darrion ran the crowbar along the top edge of the seat until it pushed through. A sliver of light shone and Vicki squealed. Darrion and Vicki pushed until the seat leaned forward an inch.

"Hold it with your feet and I'll see if I can unlatch it," Darrion said.

Vicki pushed with all her might as Darrion reached through the opening. "I found the latch, but it won't budge."

"Try the other side," Vicki gasped, trying to keep pressure on the seat.

Darrion put her arm through but couldn't reach the other side. "Let me try," Vicki said.

Footsteps approached, and the girls sat back and listened. Someone opened the front door and fumbled through the glove compartment. Another door opened and someone climbed in the backseat. "If I don't find that radio, they'll make me buy a new one."

"Maybe you put it in the trunk when you went for the gas," the other officer said.

"I don't think I even opened this trunk, but it's worth a shot. The thing's not under the seats or in the glove compartment."

The two climbed out of the car and Vicki's heart raced. Darrion grabbed the crowbar as the officer jangled his keys.

SIX

Zeke's Trouble

Vicki found the fire extinguisher and angled it toward the back of the trunk. The officer inserted the key, then cursed and fumbled with the others. Darrion quickly put the crowbar against the mechanism and snapped a wire.

The man inserted the key, turned it, but nothing happened. He did it again and again, but the trunk didn't open. "This is weird. I know this is the right key."

"Curt has a set of masters to all these cars," the other man said. "Find him and you'll get your radio."

The two walked away. Darrion pushed the seat open with her feet while Vicki stuck her arm through. She strained to reach for the latch but was a few inches short.

"Push it harder!"

"It's as far as it will go."

Vicki lunged against the backseat, cracking one of the panels. She tucked her head, pushed her shoulder against the seat, and reached through. She felt the latch with the tips of her fingers and used her feet to push farther. "Another inch and I've got it," she grunted.

Darrion gave one more furious push and Vicki grabbed the latch. The seat flew forward and Darrion crawled through. Vicki followed, leaving the radio behind, and the two crept onto the floor. They pushed the seat back to its normal position.

Vicki peeked out the back window toward the building and opened the door. "Come on." They crawled out, keeping their heads down and crab walking around the door. Vicki closed it quietly and moved away from the building. When the front door to the station opened, Vicki and Darrion rolled under another squad car and lay still.

"If you used the right key, the master's not going to do you any good," a new man said. "Did you try to get in through the backseat?"

"Didn't think of that."

A door opened. "How did the seat get torn up? It wasn't that way when we drove here."

A latch clunked and the first officer shouted, "Here it is!"

"Hold it," the other man said. "Somebody's been back here. Get the chief, quick!"

Lionel thought he heard something as he was led outside the tent, but when he turned, the guard grabbed him by the shoulder and shoved him away from the opening. Lionel was surprised by the move and lost his balance, tumbling onto the asphalt. The sun had been down for hours, but the asphalt was still warm from the soaring temperatures of the day. Lionel rolled onto his side.

Someone inside shouted and Judd burst through, carrying his shirt, the IV tape still on the back of his hand.

The guard reached for Judd's arm. "You can't leave!"

"This isn't a hospital," Judd snapped, wrenching away from the guard's grip and nearly falling. "I can go when I'm ready."

Lionel stood and put one of Judd's arms around his own neck. They walked toward the palace, Judd gasping for air and putting more weight on Lionel's shoulder.

"I'm not sure if I'm really ready," Judd whispered, "but when I saw you, I knew I had to get out of there. What time is it?"

"After midnight," Lionel said. He asked Judd what had happened, and Judd told him what he could remember. Judd shuddered as they passed the statue of Carpathia, thousands of people still standing in line for the chance to worship their idol.

Lionel was excited to tell Judd about Westin, Z-Van's pilot, and that he had prayed with Lionel after seeing Nicolae come back to life. "He remembered what we had told Z-Van on the plane and said we were dead-on with our prediction."

Judd asked to rest as they moved toward the hotel. The celebration continued in the streets. Lionel and Judd exchanged information about Z-Van and considered their next move.

"Something tells me we don't want to be here when Carpathia puts his next plan into action," Judd said.

"What's that?"

"Tsion says Carpathia's going to make everyone swear loyalty to him by forcing every living soul to take some kind of mark."

"They're probably planning how they're going to do it right now."

"Which means they're also planning what they're going to do to everyone who won't take it."

Lionel shook his head. Three and a half

years had passed since the disappearances of his family and the treaty Carpathia had made with Israel. Now that Carpathia was indwelt by Satan, the gloves were off. He didn't need to hide his evil deeds. With people blindly worshiping his image, he had the world right where he wanted it. They would follow him like sheep to the slaughter, not knowing their beloved leader was evil in the flesh.

When they saw their chance, Vicki and Darrion ran from the parking lot. When they were a safe distance away they slowed to a walk.

Vicki's hair was matted with sweat. She ran her hands through it as they walked. She hadn't been in this town for so long she hardly recognized it. The earthquake had changed streets and buildings. Damaged homes had been demolished, and the town was littered with empty lots.

They stopped for a drink of water at a fueling station, and Vicki remembered Zeke's place. The girls were hungry and tired, but Vicki said once they found Zeke, they would have all the food they could eat.

They cut across lawns and through alleys. When they heard a siren, they hid. Finally,

Vicki turned down an alley, sure that Zeke's was not far away. A suspicious-looking car sat at the end of the alley near Zeke's gas station.

"Why don't we call him?" Darrion said.

"Do you have your dad's cell phone?"

Darrion shook her head. "I got rid of it when they traced your call."

The girls backtracked into a neighborhood. Neither had much money and finding a working pay phone was almost impossible.

"Let's try one of these houses," Darrion said.

Before Vicki could protest, Darrion walked up to the first house and knocked on the door. A man wearing a dirty T-shirt opened the door a few inches. "What?"

"We're with a youth project trying to find people who are skeptical about the resurrection of Potentate Carpathia," Darrion said.

"Skeptical?" the man said. "It's been all over the television the whole day. You'd have to be a fool not to believe it."

"Right, but are there any in the neighborhood here who have acted strangely? You know, still buying into Christianity?"

The man opened the screen door and looked up and down the street. When he saw no one, he scratched at his stubbly beard and said, "I don't want to get Margaret in trouble."

"She won't be," Darrion said. "We just want to talk to her."

"Well, she's been trying to get me to read this guy's Web site . . ."

"Tsion Ben-Judah?"

"Yeah, that's him."

"Lots of silly predictions, right?"

The man leaned close. "Margaret says it's not silly. She's been trying to get me to read the Bible too."

Darrion sighed. "It's one of the telltale signs. Which house does she live in?"

"Other side, three doors down. The light blue one."

"Don't tell anyone you gave us this information," Darrion said. "It's strictly between you and us."

The man went back inside as Vicki and Darrion hurried down the street. Before they reached the house, Vicki took Darrion aside. "I don't like it that we lied to that guy back there."

"I'm just trying to find someplace safe to hide."

"I know, but I feel like we used him. He needs to know the truth too."

Darrion shoved her hands into her pockets. "So if the GC ask if we're Judah-ites, we're supposed to say yes?"

Vicki looked away. "I don't have all the answers about everything we should and shouldn't do. I'm just saying I feel bad about that guy. What if we just pushed him further away from God?"

"What do you want me to do?"

"Let's talk through what we're going to do and decide together next time."

Darrion nodded and the two climbed the steps to the house. Vicki knocked loudly, and an older woman with graying hair opened the door. When she saw the marks on Darrion's and Vicki's foreheads, she hugged them both. "Come in, come in. How did you find me?"

Darrion explained about the neighbor and Vicki's concern that they had deceived the man. The woman led them to the kitchen. "I've been working on just about everybody on the block. Don't worry about him. I'll talk to him after you've gone. I'm Maggie. What are your names and what brings you here?"

Vicki and Darrion introduced themselves and quickly told Maggie their story. "We wanted to visit a friend in the area, but I saw a suspicious car in front of his place and want to make sure everything's okay."

"Would you like something to eat while you're making your call?"

"That would be great," Vicki said.

Darrion helped Maggie while Vicki looked

up Zeke's number. When she found it, she remembered there were two phone lines into the gas station. One was the regular line anyone could use and the other was a secret line that was different by only one number. Vicki dialed and let it ring until an answering machine picked up.

Hearing Zeke's voice again made Vicki smile. "It's me, just leave a message," he said on the recording.

After the beep, she said, "This is Vicki Byrne. You might not remember me—"

"Vicki?" Zeke said as the machine beeped again. He spoke quickly and didn't seem himself. "You shouldn't have called me here."

"We were headed to your place and saw—"

"Don't come near," Zeke said. "It's crawling with GC."

"They found you?"

"They arrested Dad this morning. Charged him with subversion and took him away. Ever since then there's been at least one GC car watching our place like a hawk. Anybody who comes for gas gets arrested. I've been watching them through the cameras I rigged up around the place. I didn't see it in time to warn Dad."

"Why didn't they take you?"

"I don't go outside much, and they must

not know about our underground hideout.
I'm hoping to get out after dark. I'm packing
right now."

"Okay," Vicki said, "we won't bother you."

"Hey, good job on that satellite deal. I
heard about how you guys stirred things up
with the GC."

"Hopefully we'll do more in the future."

"I'll be praying for you," Zeke said.

Judd nearly passed out as he got into the
hotel elevator. He had walked what felt like
miles and didn't think he could go another
step. Lionel helped him to the room,
propped him against the wall, and lightly
knocked on the door. Westin opened it and
helped Judd inside.

With part emotion and part exhaustion,
Judd hugged Westin. "Welcome to the
family."

Westin carried Judd to the couch and
found him a pillow. "I think Z-Van just went
to sleep. He's been banging away at his new
songs all night."

"We have to get out of here," Judd said
when he caught his breath.

"I know that," Westin said, "and I plan on
helping you. But I'd love it if you'd stick with

me for a week or two and teach me everything you know."

Judd glanced at Lionel. Since Carpathia's
rising he could think of nothing but getting
out of New Babylon and away from all the
trouble. He knew, of course, that there
would soon be trouble everywhere and
finding a hiding place would be nearly
impossible. Still, his heart ached to see the
others, especially Vicki.

"Let's talk about it after we get some rest."

Mark and the others at the abandoned bookstore rested throughout the day and waited
for nightfall. Several GC cars passed, but the
kids stayed hidden. When evening came and
the sun began its slow descent over the hillside, Mark smelled smoke and wondered
how close the fire would come to the lake.

As soon as it was dark, Mark pulled
Conrad aside and asked him to come with
him. He told the others they would be back
soon and to be ready.

Mark and Conrad slipped through the
quiet streets until they came to the old
library. A tow truck was parked along the
bank, a few yards from where the car had
plunged into the water.

"Doesn't look like they've pulled the Suburban out yet," Conrad said.

"That's what I was hoping," Mark said as he took off his shirt and shoes.

"What are you doing?"

"We need cash. We don't have much of a chance without it."

"You heard Vicki's last count," Conrad said. "There's maybe a hundred Nicks left down there in the cash box."

"That's a hundred more than we have right now, and I'm going to get it."

"What about the tow-truck operator?"

"Distract him," Mark said. "I'll swing around and get in the water up the beach. You keep him busy."

Conrad shook his head. "I'm not very good at that stuff. Let me do the dive. I'm a stronger swimmer."

Mark agreed and put his clothes back on. Conrad ran up the beach a few hundred yards, and Mark walked toward the tow truck. A man sat inside smoking a cigarette. Yellow tape wound around the site where the Suburban had gone into the water.

"How's it goin'?" Mark said as he stepped up to the truck.

"It'll go a lot better for you if you get out of here. GC doesn't want anybody bothering this place until they can get a bigger rig to pull that car out."

"So one really did go in, huh? I didn't know whether to believe it or not."

"Believe it and get out of here. Besides, I just heard on the radio that the fire's only about three miles away. You should have been evacuated a long time ago."

Mark noticed Conrad slipping up to the pier and heading out in the water. "I didn't know it was that close. Why are they making you stay?"

"I told you, to keep everybody away from this site."

"Who was in the car?"

"A bunch of kids. Now leave me alone before I call the GC."

Mark held up his hands. "Just curious. Didn't mean to bother you."

Mark stepped away and looked at the water. Conrad surfaced and Mark coughed to cover the noise. "Smoke's getting close. I'll be seeing you."

"Yeah," the man said.

A few minutes later Conrad returned to the library holding a box and the shoe he had wedged onto the accelerator. "Couldn't see a thing down there. It took me a couple of dives to find the car, but once I got inside, it was easy." He opened the box and picked up the soaked cash.

"We'll count it back at the bookstore," Mark said. "Come on."

Vicki and Darrion explained what they had been through since the disappearances. Maggie listened with interest, covering her mouth when Darrion told of the deaths of her father and mother.

Vicki described Charlie and the couple he had stayed with. "They're in GC custody now, but we have someone on the inside who said she'd help get them out."

Maggie bit her lip. "First thing you need is a good night's rest."

"What about your story?" Darrion said.

The woman smiled. "In the morning. Let me get you some nightclothes."

Vicki awoke from a dead sleep a few hours later. A thunderous explosion rocked the neighborhood and a plume of fire and smoke shot hundreds of feet into the air. Vicki and Darrion changed into their clothes and ran outside. They wound their way through the neighborhood until they reached the fire. Vicki's heart sank. Zeke's gas station was completely engulfed in flames.

SEVEN

Maggie's Story

MARK led the way back to the bookstore in the soft glow of the moon. The smoke was getting thicker and his eyes stung. They were only a block away from the hideout when a GC vehicle passed slowly, its lights flashing. Mark and Conrad ducked out of sight.

"Attention: all residents are to leave immediately. This is a forced evacuation. For your own safety, exit the city and go east. The wildfire has jumped the fire line over the main road. Again, exit quickly and orderly."

When the car passed, Mark and Conrad raced to the bookstore and found the others. Shelly was angry that they took the risk but grateful they had money.

Conrad pulled a wad of cash from his pocket and counted the Nicks. They had more than two hundred, which wouldn't buy them a car, but it would be enough for food.

"You don't think this is a trick to lure us out?" Melinda said.

"The smoke's enough to convince me," Mark said.

Cars jammed the main road out of town. The five stayed out of sight as much as possible, slowly finding their way through woods and farmland that ran parallel to the road. Shelly suggested they follow the lake and look for a campsite.

"This whole place is going up," Conrad said, pointing behind them. In the distance flames licked at the tops of trees and moved toward the town.

Janie shook her head as they walked through a field of tall grass. "I don't understand any of this."

"What do you mean?" Shelly said.

"Vicki and Darrion are lost or were taken by the GC, and we're running from a wildfire with no place to stay and not much money. Charlie and the Shairtons are locked up in some holding tank in Des Plaines. Why would God let us go through all this if we believe in him?"

"Just because you believe in God and accept his forgiveness doesn't mean you don't have trouble," Shelly said.

"Yeah, think about Jesus' friends," Conrad said. "They just wanted to follow God and tell people the Good News. Most of them were killed because of what they believed."

Janie rolled her eyes. "That's comforting."

"Believers have gone through tough things all along," Shelly said. "Sometimes becoming a Christian gets them in trouble with their family. Friends turn their backs. The government cracks down on them or they have a hard time at their jobs. Trouble doesn't mean God's abandoned you or that he isn't in control. He promises to go through the hard times with you."

"But what's the point?" Janie said. "Wouldn't it be a lot easier if we just went along with the GC until Jesus comes back?"

"God never promised easy," Conrad said. "From the time I first believed until now, it's been a struggle. My brother's dead, all the family and friends I've known are gone, but it's still worth it."

"Why?"

"Because the Bible is coming true every day. God is real. He keeps his promises. We could hide in some cave, but I don't think that's what God wants us to do."

Janie stopped and turned away from the others. "Even though I can see things coming true, like Carpathia rising from the dead, I still don't understand."

Shelly put an arm around Janie. "I learned from Vicki a long time ago that we'll always have questions and doubts. That you struggle with them is proof that your faith is working on you. God is making your faith more real every day. He's preparing you for something."

Janie looked up with tears in her eyes. "You really think so?"

Shelly nodded. "There's a verse in Jeremiah that says God knows the plans he has for you. 'They are plans for good and not for disaster, to give you a future and a hope.' "

Janie smiled and the two walked together. Mark led the kids into the night. They all prayed for Vicki and Darrion as they went.

Vicki awoke the next morning to the smell of a home-cooked breakfast. She let Darrion sleep and stumbled to the kitchen table. Eggs and bacon sizzled in a skillet.

"I took a walk this morning and looked at that gas station," Maggie said. "There's nothing left but a big hole in the ground."

Vicki noticed an old computer in the corner of the room and asked if it still worked.

Maggie nodded. "I mostly used it to write

my grandkids before the disappearances.
Now I read what Tsion Ben-Judah says and
keep up with the news. You can use it if
you'd like."

Vicki logged on to the kids' Web site and
gasped at the hundreds of e-mails that had
piled up without being answered. She
quickly typed a message to Mark and the
others saying she and Darrion were okay. She
gave them the bad news about Zeke's father
and the gas station. *I don't know about Zeke,
but it doesn't look good,* she wrote. *I hope you
get this and that you're all right.*

She sent the e-mail and scanned the
incoming messages. She recognized Natalie's
address and quickly pulled up her e-mail.

> *Vicki, where are you? There was a big
> commotion last night about someone break-
> ing into a GC car that had been up to
> Wisconsin. Do you know anything about it?*
>
> *I found out more about Charlie and the
> Shairtons. They're still here being ques-
> tioned. The GC had watched the farmhouse
> after they found the satellite truck a few
> miles away. When you didn't show up, they
> moved in and arrested Charlie and the
> Shairtons.*
>
> *They've brought in another man on
> charges of subversion, and I think that's*

*what they'll charge the Shairtons with.
They've moved Charlie to a separate holding area, so I think if we're going to get him
out, we'd better do it soon.*

*I hope you get this message and that
you're okay. If I don't hear from you soon,
I'll try something myself.*

Love,
Natalie

Vicki quickly typed back: *Darrion and I are
in Des Plaines. We hitched a ride in the GC's
trunk without them knowing it. We're ready to
help. Have you heard anything about Mark and
the others? Give a safe phone number where I
can call you. And be careful, Natalie. These guys
mean business. Love, Vicki.*

"Your breakfast is ready anytime," Maggie
said.

Darrion walked in rubbing her eyes, and
the three sat at the table. Maggie offered to
pray. "Lord, you know our needs better than
we do, and we thank you for giving us this
food. We're going to enjoy it and the days we
have left before your return. Protect Vicki,
Darrion, and their friends and give them
what they need. In Jesus' name, amen."

Vicki and Darrion ate hungrily. Vicki could
tell from the meal the night before that

Maggie was a good cook, but breakfast was even better.

"What's your story?" Darrion said.

Maggie spread jam on a piece of toast and sat back. "I've been a widow for almost ten years. Before that, my husband and I were agnostics. You know what that means?"

"That you don't know whether God exists or not," Vicki said.

"Right. We didn't think there was really enough evidence. My husband taught science at a community college so we were big on proving things. We didn't vote for anyone who couldn't prove they'd do a good job. We didn't buy products that didn't live up to their promises, that kind of thing.

"Our children were raised that way too. Twins—a boy and a girl. But something went wrong when they got to college. They got mixed up with this campus group of Christians, and the next thing you know, the kids are home trying to convert us."

"What did you and your husband do?" Darrion said.

"We listened, of course, but we believed they'd been brainwashed. Finally, we told them it was all right with us if they wanted to throw away their minds, but they should stop trying to change ours."

"What did they do?"

"They stopped. They didn't mention God or Jesus or the Bible one more time, so I thought it was something they'd snap out of. But when they both got married to Christians, I realized they were committed."

"They never talked about it again?" Vicki said.

"They didn't have to," Maggie said. "They lived it. They showed a love to their kids I'd never seen. They were there for me when Don died—that's my husband. Sometimes I'd wonder if I could have what they had, but I'd push the thought away. It was too painful to think that Don and I had missed out on the greatest truth of the universe."

"What happened?" Darrion said.

"The Rapture. I had e-mailed my granddaughter something the night before. She always got up early and wrote back. It was exciting to read her notes every morning.

"Well, there was no message that day. I didn't think much about it until I turned on the news and saw what was going on. I was devastated to learn that my whole family was gone. My kids had never talked about the Rapture, but I knew this had something to do with God."

"That's when you saw Tsion Ben-Judah?" Vicki said.

"No, that's when I picked up a Bible off the shelf and started reading." Maggie closed her eyes. "I read the New Testament straight through in a couple of days. When I got to Romans, I finally understood that the proof I had been looking for was right under my nose. Jesus had made such a difference in the lives of my kids. If he did rise from the dead and do all those miracles, what more did I need?

"I asked God to forgive my hard heart and change me. And he did. It was sometime later that I came across Tsion Ben-Judah and his writings."

Maggie asked what Vicki had found on the computer, and Vicki told her everything about the Young Tribulation Force. Vicki logged on again and found a message from Natalie that included a phone number.

Hurry, Natalie wrote.

Lionel let Judd sleep most of the next day. He called a few airlines about commercial flights to the States. Several companies reported that flights into New Babylon had been full before the funeral, but flights out had been nearly empty.

"Everybody wanted to get here for the

memorial service," one attendant said, "and now nobody wants to leave."

Lionel found a flight that would get them close to Chicago. It was more money than he and Judd had, but a good option, especially considering Z-Van's deepening loyalty to Carpathia.

Lionel decided to wait and talk with Judd before going ahead with the plan.

Mark awoke in a school that had been converted into an emergency shelter. Earlier that morning he and the others had split up before going inside, not wanting to attract attention. He had been given some bedding, a number, and was pointed down a long hallway to the gymnasium. The gym floor was littered with sleeping bags, mattresses, and old cots. Those who couldn't afford hotel rooms farther away had moved frantically east to this spot.

Mark noticed Conrad on the other side of the gym and gave him a nod. Conrad returned the greeting and lay down on his cot.

Women slept in classrooms while men stayed in the gym. There were a few teenage boys present, but most were married men whose families were sleeping in a classroom.

Mark looked for any other believers as he walked to the bathroom. He overheard two men talking about the fire. The GC had reported that the wind had switched directions just before it reached Lake Geneva and that the town might be saved.

"I'll bet if Carpathia were here he'd be able to stop the fire in no time," one man said. "You saw what happened. This man is god!"

When he returned to his cot, Mark took the laptop from under his covers and looked for a power outlet. He found one near Conrad's cot.

Mark made small talk with Conrad, as if they had just met, and pulled up the kids' Web site. He let Conrad read Vicki's message, and they were both relieved to know the girls were safe.

"That makes our job easier," Conrad whispered.

"How's that?"

"We don't have to look for Charlie and the Shairtons. We simply find a place they can bring them."

Mark agreed and wrote Vicki about it. He also sent a quick message to Judd and Lionel in case they returned to the country and didn't know where to find the Young Trib Force.

"I'll go tell the others the good news," Conrad said.

"Get ready to leave," Mark said. "The GC could inspect this place anytime."

Mark looked at the hundreds of e-mails that had come in during the last two days. So many kids had questions. The unbelievers were mostly anxious and afraid. A few scolded the kids and praised Nicolae Carpathia as god. But the believers simply wanted to know Carpathia's next move and how they should prepare.

As Mark thought about what he could say, he noticed an e-mail from Tsion Ben-Judah. He opened it quickly and read:

> *Dear Mark,*
> *I am sending the following letter so you can relay it to kids around the world. I trust you to make my words easy to understand for your readers. There is no longer any question about Nicolae Carpathia. I am persuaded that Leon is his false prophet. Those who have ears will not be deceived, but they must hear this message.*
>
> *I pray for you and the rest of the Young Tribulation Force every day. You do not know what an incredible impact you are having. Keep up the good work, and may God give you the courage you need to stand*

for him in this difficult time. Remember,
even though Satan now indwells Carpathia,
greater is he who is in you, than he who is
in the world!
Your friend,
Tsion Ben-Judah

Mark smiled. Tsion didn't know it, but he
had just given Mark the very thing he needed
to answer the hundreds of e-mails in front of
him.

EIGHT

Tsion's Letter

JUDD awoke with a pounding headache. Lionel stood over him and placed a few sheets of paper on his bed. "Feeling well enough for some good news?"

Judd sat up and winced. "Tell me."

Lionel explained what Mark had written about Vicki and the others. Though the kids were separated, they were all accounted for. The only ones in immediate danger, it seemed, were Charlie and the farm couple who had befriended the kids in Illinois, the Shairtons. "Oh, Zeke's dad was arrested too."

"What's this?" Judd said, picking up the papers.

"Mark's translation of Tsion Ben-Judah's latest letter. It's long, but he answers a lot in here."

Lionel brought some food and water, and

Judd propped himself up with a few pillows. He drank in every word from Dr. Ben-Judah.

> *To: The beloved tribulation saints scattered throughout the earth, believers in the one true Jehovah God and his matchless Son, Jesus the Christ, our Savior and Lord*

> *From: Your servant, Tsion Ben-Judah, blessed by the Lord with the privilege of teaching you, under the authority of his Holy Spirit, from the Bible, the very Word of God*

> *Re: The dawn of the Great Tribulation*

> *My dear brothers and sisters in Christ, As is so often true when I write you, I come in both joy and sorrow, delighted yet sober in spirit. Forgive the delay since I last wrote, and thank you all for your concern for me. My comrades and I are safe and praising the Lord for a new base of operations. And I always want to thank God for the miracle of technology that allows me to write to you all over the world.*

> *Though I have met few of you personally and look forward to that one day, either in the kingdom Christ sets up after his return or in heaven, I feel we are drawn together like a family as we share the riches of Scrip-*

ture in these letters. Thank you for your prayers that I will remain faithful to my calling and healthy enough to continue for as long as the Father himself gives me breath.

Tsion wrote that readership of his Web site had passed the one-billion mark. Though the Global Community denied the figures, Judd knew it was true. Dr. Ben-Judah revealed the process he went through for interpreting prophecy. Judd knew if this letter reached those who were undecided about God, many could be persuaded about the truth.

While the prophecies that foretold Messiah were fairly straightforward and led me to believe in Jesus as their unique fulfillment, I prayed that God would reveal the key to the rest of the prophecies. He did this by impressing upon me to take the words as literally as I took any others from the Bible, unless the context and the wording itself indicated otherwise.

In other words, I had always taken at its word a passage such as "Love your neighbor as yourself," or "Do for others what you would like them to do for you." Why then, could I not take literally a verse which said that John, the writer of Revelation, saw a pale horse? Yes, I understood that the horse stood for something. And yet the Bible said that John saw it. I took that literally, along with all the other prophetic statements (unless they used phrases such as "like unto" or others that made it clear they were symbolic).

Judd had to go back over Tsion's words a second time, but he finally understood. Tsion's straightforward reading of the Bible helped the teacher discover the order of the Seal and Trumpet Judgments and that the Bowl Judgments yet to come would be even worse than those they had witnessed.

Believers, we have turned a corner. Skeptics—and I know many of you drop in to see what we are up to—we have passed the point of politeness. Until now, I have been direct about the Bible but somewhat cautious about the current rulers of this world.

No more. As every prophecy in the Bible has so far come true, as the leader of this world has preached peace while swinging a sword, as he died by the sword and was resurrected as the Scriptures foretold, and as his right-hand man has been given similar evil power, there can be no more doubt:

Nicolae Carpathia, the so-called Excellency and Supreme Potentate of the Global Community, is both anti-Christian and Antichrist himself. And the Bible says the resurrected Antichrist is literally indwelt by Satan himself. Leon Fortunato, who had an image of Antichrist erected and now forces all to worship it or face death, is Antichrist's false prophet. As the Bible predicted, he has power to make the statue speak and to call down fire from heaven to destroy those who refuse to worship it.

What's next? Consider this clear prophetic passage in Revelation 13:11-18: "Then I saw another beast come up out of the earth. He had two horns like those of a lamb, and he spoke with the voice of a dragon. He exercised all the authority of the first beast. And he required all the earth and those who belong to this world to worship the first beast, whose death-wound had been healed.

"He did astounding miracles, such as making fire flash down to earth from heaven while everyone was watching. And with all the miracles he was allowed to perform on behalf of the first beast, he deceived all the people who belong to this world. He ordered the people of the world to

make a great statue of the first beast, who was fatally wounded and then came back to life.

"He was permitted to give life to this statue so that it could speak. Then the statue commanded that anyone refusing to worship it must die. He required everyone—great and small, rich and poor, slave and free—to be given a mark on the right hand or on the forehead. And no one could buy or sell anything without that mark, which was either the name of the beast or the number representing his name.

"Wisdom is needed to understand this. Let the one who has understanding solve the number of the beast, for it is the number of a man. His number is 666."

It won't be long before everyone will be forced to bow the knee to Carpathia or his image, to bear his name or number on their forehead or right hand, or face the consequences.

Those consequences? The Bible calls this the mark of the beast. Those without it will not be allowed to legally buy or sell. If we publicly refuse to accept the mark of the beast, we will be beheaded. While it is the greatest desire of my life to live to see the Glorious Appearing of Jesus Christ at the end of the Great Tribulation (a few days

> *short of three and a half years from now),*
> *what greater cause could there ever be for*
> *which to give one's life?*
>
> *Many, millions of us, will be required to*
> *do just that.*

Judd put the page down and closed his eyes. To think of millions of believers losing their lives because they wouldn't obey Carpathia was almost unbelievable. How would the Global Community carry out so many executions? Would Judd be asked to give his life?

Judd read the next few sentences which included Tsion's belief that every believer called on to give his or her life would be given strength by God to endure the beheading. Tsion also wrote that taking the mark would forever condemn a person to eternity without God.

> *While many will live in secret, supporting*
> *one another through private markets, some*
> *will find themselves caught and dragged*
> *into a public beheading. To live, the only*
> *alternative is to reject Christ and take the*
> *mark of the beast.*
>
> *If you are already a believer, you will not*
> *be able to turn your back on Christ, praise*
> *God. If you are undecided and don't want*

to follow the crowd, what will you do when faced with the mark or the loss of your head? I plead with you today to believe, to receive Christ, and cover yourself with protection from God.

We are entering the bloodiest season in the history of the world. Those who take the mark of the beast will suffer at the hand of God. Those who refuse it will be killed for his blessed cause. Never has the choice been so stark, so clear.

God himself named this three-and-a-half-year period. Matthew 24:21-22 records Jesus saying, "For that will be a time of greater horror than anything the world has ever seen or will ever see again. In fact, unless that time of calamity is shortened, the entire human race will be destroyed. But it will be shortened for the sake of God's chosen ones."

In all God's dealings with humans, this is the shortest period on record, and yet more Scripture is devoted to it than any other period except the life of Christ. The Hebrew prophets spoke of this as a time of God's revenge for the slaughter of the prophets and saints over the centuries. But it is also a time of mercy. God compresses the decision-making time for men and *women before the coming of Christ to set up his earthly kingdom.*

This is clearly the most awful time in history, but I still say it is also a merciful act of God to give as many as possible an opportunity to put their faith in Christ. Oh, people, we are the army of God with a massive job to do in a short time. May we be willing and eager to show the courage that comes only from him. There are countless lost souls in need of saving, and we have the truth.

It may be hard to recognize God's mercy when his wrath is also increasing. Woe to those who believe the lie that God is only "love." Yes, he is love. And his gift of Jesus as the sacrifice for our sin is the greatest evidence of this. But the Bible also says God is "holy, holy, holy." He is righteous and a God of justice, and it is not in his nature to allow sin to go unpunished or unpaid for.

We are engaged in a great worldwide battle with Satan himself for the souls of men and women. I do not say this lightly, for I do understand the power of the evil one. But I have placed my faith and trust in the God who sits high above the heavens, in the God who is above all other gods, and among whom there is none like him.

Scripture is clear that you can test both

prophet and prophecy. I make no claim of being a prophet, but I believe the prophecies. If they are not true and don't come to pass, then I am a liar and the Bible is bogus, and we are all utterly without hope. But if the Bible is true, next on the agenda is the ceremonial desecration (or defiling) of the temple in Jerusalem by Antichrist himself. This is a prediction made by Daniel, Jesus, Paul, and John.

Tsion wrote specifically to Jewish readers and prepared them for what was to come in Jerusalem. Nicolae would go into the holy temple and sacrifice a pig on the sacred altar.

If you are Jewish and have not yet been persuaded that Jesus the Christ of Nazareth is Messiah and you have been deceived by the lies of Nicolae Carpathia, perhaps your mind will be changed when he breaks his covenant with Israel and withdraws his guarantee of her safety.

But he shows no favoritism. Besides reviling the Jews, he will slaughter believers in Jesus.

If this does not happen, label me a heretic or mad and look elsewhere than the Holy Scriptures for hope.

Thank you for your patience and for the

*blessed privilege of communicating with you
again. Let me leave you on a note of hope.
My next message will concern the difference
between the Book of Life and the Lamb's
Book of Life, and what those mean to you
and me. Until then, you may rest assured
that if you are a believer and have placed
your hope and trust in the work of Jesus
Christ alone for the forgiveness of sins and
for life everlasting, your name is in the
Lamb's Book of Life.*

And it can never be erased.

*Until we meet again, I bless you in the
name of Jesus. May he bless you and keep
you and make his face to shine upon you,
and give you peace.*

Judd stared at the wall. So this was it. Everything was out in the open. Tsion Ben-Judah
hadn't held back anything about Carpathia.

"What do you think?" Lionel said.

Judd sighed. "I think what we've already
been through will seem easy compared—"

The door opened and Westin walked in.
"Z-Van just got off the phone with someone
from Carpathia's office. They've asked him to
go to Jerusalem for another celebration."

Judd gripped the pages. "What's the celebration for?"

"They told Z-Van they were going to give true worship to Carpathia and deal with his enemies."

Judd nodded and looked at Lionel. Tsion's words were already coming true.

NINE

Changing Course

VICKI dialed Natalie's number but got a GC answering machine. She hung up and tried a few minutes later, again getting the machine. More than an hour later, a man answered.

"I'm looking for Natalie Bishop," Vicki said.

"Sorry, not in this department."

"She gave me this number."

The man sighed and clicked a few keys on a computer. "She's been reassigned. What do you want with her?"

"She's a friend of mine and—"

"She's not here. If you want to leave a message—"

"What's her new assignment?"

"Corrections. I know there's been a lot of activity down there. Now, if you don't mind—"

"Can you transfer me?"

"Miss, this is not a chat room. If it's not official GC business, I suggest you contact her on her personal time."

"Okay, can you tell me when—"

Click.

Vicki told Darrion what she had learned, and the two agreed to wait for Natalie to get in touch. Darrion handed Vicki a sheet of paper she had printed from the kids' Web site. It was a new message from Tsion Ben-Judah.

Mark wanted to show the others Tsion's letter, but they didn't dare stay at the school with the GC so close. Mark kicked himself for not getting out earlier and asked Conrad to round up the rest of the group and meet behind the school near a tree. He walked past new arrivals in the gymnasium, trying to find anyone with the mark of loyalty to Christ. There was no one.

The others emerged from the school one at a time, just as Mark had suggested. Shelly and the others said they hadn't noticed any believers in the women's area.

"Before we leave, I think you ought to know what we're up against," Mark said. He opened the computer and read every word Tsion Ben-Judah had written. The kids were quiet as Mark read, and the further he went, the more concerned they looked.

"Well, if Tsion wasn't on Carpathia's most-wanted list before, he's there now," Conrad said.

"Can you believe Fortunato is the false prophet?" Shelly said.

"What's that mean?" Janie said.

"Basically the Antichrist's vice president," Conrad said.

Melinda scratched her head. "What's the thing about the image?"

"You know, the statue at the funeral," Mark said. "My guess is they're going to cart it around and make people worship it."

Conrad shook his head. "They'll probably mass produce them and have one in every town."

"What's that stuff about the right hand and 666?" Janie said.

"Remember how we talked about Satan counterfeiting everything God does? Well, he's doing it again. Satan's plan is to destroy as many people as he can, so he's making everyone take his mark on the hand or forehead. If you want to buy or sell something, you have to have the mark."

"Then believers are going to starve to death!" Janie said.

"That's why Chloe Williams and the others put together the commodity co-op. They've been storing food and supplies so believers won't starve. People like Zeke and Pete have helped get it where it's needed most. Hopefully, it will be enough to last."

"I used to know a guy who thought his social security number was the mark of the beast," Conrad said. "Guess he was wrong."

"So if we don't take the mark, they cut off our heads?" Janie said.

Shelly shuddered. "What an awful way to die. And there will be millions."

"I don't know if I could do it," Melinda said. "I mean, I know Dr. Ben-Judah says God will help us, but what if we crack?"

"They'll give you a choice between worshiping Carpathia or worshiping God," Conrad said. "Unless that seal on your forehead is fake, God won't let you make the wrong choice."

"Plus, they have to catch us," Mark said.

"I guess there's good news in all of this," Shelly said. "People still have time to choose God. After they take the mark, they won't have a choice."

"Which means we have to tell readers on the Web site to be bold," Mark said.

Janie stood and turned her back on the

group. She walked a few steps toward the school.

"What's wrong?" Shelly said.

Janie put a hand to her face and shook her head. "If Dr. Ben-Judah is right, and I believe he is, the people in that school are going to take Carpathia's mark and they'll suffer." Janie turned and wiped away a tear. "I don't want to be caught by the GC, and I sure don't want them to chop my head off. But we ought to tell these people the truth rather than run away from them."

"Let's take a vote," Mark said. "Who wants to get out of here right now and find a place to hide?"

No one moved.

"Who wants to tell these people the truth about God?"

Everyone raised a hand and Mark smiled. "Then we'd better pray and get to it."

In the afternoon, Vicki and Darrion watched news of people's reaction to Nicolae Carpathia's resurrection. Thousands still waited in line in New Babylon for their chance to worship the statue. There was talk of constructing other statues in different parts of the world.

Religious experts said the world had never seen such a widely exposed miracle. "This godlike display of power can only be compared to the mythical accounts of the Bible," one expert said. "In those stories, the miracles were only viewed by a few people. This one was seen all over the world at the same time."

"That's not true," Darrion said. "Lots of people saw the miracles in the Bible, didn't they?"

Vicki nodded.

Maggie yelled when an e-mail came in from Natalie that included a new phone number.

Natalie answered on the first ring and took the phone into another room. "I have a roommate who's true-blue Carpathia."

"What happened?"

"My transfer to corrections came through after I sent the first message."

"Have you seen Charlie and the Shairtons?"

"I saw Charlie today but didn't talk with him. I don't want him to know about any of this until it's time. The Shairtons are in the adult groups, but they're okay."

"Have they brought in more people?"

"An older guy yesterday who ran a rebel gas station."

"That's Zeke!" Vicki said.

"How did you know he was named Zeke?"

Vicki told Natalie the story of the gas station and how Zeke and his father had helped them.

"They think the guy is part of a conspiracy against the GC. They arrested anybody who stopped at his station to buy gas."

"How many?" Vicki said.

"About ten are still in custody. But most of them just saw that his station was open and stopped for gas."

"What's the plan?" Vicki said.

Natalie had several ideas and told Vicki all of them. Vicki thought they were all too dangerous.

After a few minutes, Natalie said she needed to go because her roommate wanted to use the phone. "One more thing. Our division received a message from GC headquarters in New Babylon. They said they're producing loyalty enforcement facilitators."

"What's that?" Vicki said.

"Guillotines, as in chop your head off."

"That's awful."

"The message said each sector of the United Carpathian States should have them up and cutting within thirty days."

"Hopefully we won't be anywhere near when that happens."

"I'll call or e-mail you from work tomorrow."

Vicki hung up and told Darrion the ideas. When Vicki finished, Maggie scooted her chair closer. "If you get those people out of jail, they'll be in more trouble than they're in now. If they don't charge them, the GC might let them go."

"With those guillotines on their way, we can't take that chance," Darrion said.

"You need to be willing to get thrown in jail yourself before you do this."

"We are," Vicki said.

Maggie smiled, a twinkle in her eyes. "So am I. Let me help."

Mark and the others went back inside the school. A GC sponsored relief organization provided sandwiches and drinks for lunch. The kids decided to split up and talk with people individually. Mark sat by a man and his teenage son and asked where they lived.

"A couple of miles on the other side of the lake," the man said. "I thought we'd be okay once the fiery hail burned a bunch of trees a while back. Now this."

"I'd like to get my hands on the people who started the fire," the boy said.

The man said he had lost everything he had in life, except the clothes on his back, the truck parked outside, and his son.

"Were you married?" Mark said.

"Divorced," the man said. "My ex fought it the whole way, but I had to be free. She got custody of the kids. Then all of them disappeared, except for Quin here."

The boy looked at his father. "I like living with my dad. Don't have to go to church every week and do all that stupid religious stuff."

Mark nodded, frustrated that the conversation wasn't going better. He wanted to show them Tsion's letter or stand on tables and shout the truth to everyone. These two needed God, but Mark couldn't force them to believe. "You ever think about all the stuff that's happened and wonder why?"

"All the time," the father said. "And I think we got our answer."

"Really?"

"Yeah, all of this has been for a purpose, to show that Nicolae Carpathia really is a god."

"If we ever get enough money," Quin said, "I want to go to New Babylon and see where he came back to life."

Mark excused himself and threw away his trash. Conrad joined him, also discouraged with the people he had talked with.

Janie ran to them with a thin young woman holding a baby. "Terry, these are the guys I was telling you about. They helped me understand."

Mark and Conrad shook hands with the woman and sat at a table in the back of the room. "How can we help you?" Mark said.

"I'm scared for my child. I used to think there was a God, but now I'm not sure."

Mark leaned over the table. "There is a God and even in the middle of all this ugliness, he loves you."

"Really?"

Janie moved across the room and talked with an older man. Mark turned back to Terry and asked if he could tell her some things about the Bible.

"The Bible talks about this? I thought it just listed the things you shouldn't do."

Mark opened his computer and showed Terry verses that predicted what they had experienced the past three years. Terry read each word and seemed eager to hear more.

"Jesus said that he came so that people could have life, and have it to the full. Most people are either living just to stay alive or they're following Nicolae Carpathia."

"I just want a safe place for me and my baby."

"I understand," Mark said, "but what if I told you that you can know real safety and have a lasting peace in your heart?"

"What do you mean?"

Mark explained sin and that a holy God can't accept anything that's not perfect. "That's why Jesus was born. He was God in the flesh. He lived a perfect life and was sacrificed so that you and I could be forgiven and live forever with God."

The baby cried and Terry held it close. "I know I've done bad things, but I want to be forgiven. I want peace."

Mark thought of Tsion Ben-Judah's words. "You need to know that if you choose God, those who hate God are going to be against you."

"What does that mean? I thought you said I would be safe."

"You'll be safe from the judgments God is pouring out, but God's enemies might try to hurt you."

The baby screamed and Terry stood. "Let me think about it."

TEN

Natalie's Plan

MARK talked with people until a GC official arrived and called everyone together in the gymnasium. A janitor plugged a microphone into a wall jack, and the man's voice was amplified through small speakers.

"There's good news for a lot of you," the official said. "It looks like the fire missed Lake Geneva."

People whooped and yelled, giving each other high fives. Quin and his father didn't celebrate.

"The wind changed direction and it's blowing the opposite way. We've counted about two dozen homes in the forest that didn't make it. Those people will be eligible for assistance through the Global Community."

The officer said those who lived near town might be able to return home in the morning. "But we'd like your help locating those we think started the fire." The man held up a picture of Vicki. "We think this girl and some others were involved. They are religious zealots and if you have any information, please see me. People rushed up to the man when he was finished, asking questions about their homes and the GC assistance.

Mark and everyone but Shelly slipped away together. Each of the kids reported they had talked with a few people but that no one had prayed.

Shelly rushed up to the group. "A couple just drove up in a big van. They have the mark of the believer and said we could stay with them."

"Where do they live?" Conrad said.

"On a farm east of here. They heard about the emergency shelter and brought some food."

Mark quickly met the man and his wife and explained what they were doing. "We'll wait here until you're ready to go," the man said.

"Are there any more GC people around?" Mark said to the others.

"They just left," Shelly said.

"Then everybody get your stuff together. Conrad, grab the laptop."

"But what about these people?" Janie said. "We haven't talked to all of them."

Mark put a hand on Janie's shoulder. "We'll take care of that right now."

Mark approached the janitor, who was unplugging the microphone. "I want to say something. Could you wait?"

The janitor nodded and stood to the side, his arms folded.

"If I could have your attention," Mark said into the microphone. The room hushed and Mark began to sweat. He cleared his throat as people looked at him. "My friends and I have been talking with some of you about what's happened the past three years. We've found something that's made sense, and we'd like to share it with any of you who want to listen."

"What are you talking about?" a woman in the back yelled.

"By listening to people who know the Bible, we believe that what happened in New Babylon was predicted a long time ago. And things are going to get worse."

"Hey, pal," Quin's father said, "Carpathia just rose from the dead. I'd say that's a good thing."

"That depends on what you believe about Carpathia. If we're right, he'll make everybody worship him and take some kind of identifier on their forehead or their right hand."

"Why shouldn't we worship him?" Quin's father said. "If he can come back from the dead he has to be god."

"Let the kid talk," someone said.

"Fine, but I get my say too! For all we know, this guy set the fire."

Mark looked nervously around the room. He hadn't planned on starting a debate; he simply wanted to tell people the truth. Now all eyes were on him. "If you want to follow Carpathia, that's your decision. But if you feel like there's something wrong with the whole Global Community, please come up front."

Mark moved away from the microphone and thanked the janitor. The room buzzed with conversation, some asking who these kids were, others getting their cots ready for bed. A few came forward.

The first person who reached Mark was Terry, the woman with the baby. "I've thought a lot about what you said earlier," she said. "I don't care what the GC do to me. I need God to forgive me."

Mark smiled. Conrad, Shelly, and Janie came to the front. Quickly, Mark went through the information he had shared with Terry. "Anyone who wants to pray right now, come with me."

Terry and three others joined Mark in the corner. The janitor still stood with his arms crossed, one foot on the side of the wall.

"Pray with me. God, I'm sorry for my sin, and I want to turn from it right now and accept the gift you're offering me. I believe that Jesus died on the cross and paid the penalty for my sin. I accept your offer of mercy and grace, and I ask you to come into my heart and make me a new person. Change me from the inside out."

The people next to Mark prayed the prayer out loud with him. Mark concluded: "I thank you for saving me from my sin, and I ask you to be the Lord of my life from this day on until you come again. Give me the strength to live for you. In Jesus' name, amen."

Mark looked at Terry and smiled. On her forehead was the mark of the believer. The others around her had the mark as well and they asked what it was for. As Mark explained, he noticed the smiling janitor had a mark too.

Melinda rushed forward and grabbed Mark's arm. "They're onto us. I just heard a man calling the GC on his cell phone."

Mark went to the group of new believers and held up a hand. "I'm sorry to cut this short, but we're in danger. We have to leave.

If you prayed and you want to go with us, come now."

The kids gathered their things and headed outside.

A man in the back yelled, "Stop! I've got some questions!"

"That's the one," Shelly whispered.

"Sorry," Mark yelled at the man, "maybe another time."

Mark pushed the others out a side door. The janitor followed with a broom and stuck it through the handle. Someone on the inside pounded on the door and shouted.

"Go!" the janitor said. "I'll take care of the GC."

Mark shook hands with the man and ran to the waiting van. As it pulled away, Mark and the rest of the passengers saw flashing lights coming from town. The driver of the van turned off his headlights and drove the other way. A few miles later they crested a hill, and the man turned onto a dirt road that led into the countryside.

"Don't worry, kids," the driver said. "The GC won't find you now."

Vicki awoke early the next morning and helped Maggie make breakfast. She pulled up the kids' Web site, but there was no word from Natalie. She found a message from Mark sent late the night before. He explained about their time at the emergency shelter and talking with people about God.

Last night we met some believers who have an awesome hideout, Mark wrote. *We brought some people we had met at the shelter, and every one of them has decided to follow God!*

The people here are willing to help us in any way. They said they'd even come to Des Plaines and help spring Charlie and the Shairtons. I'll tell you more about them later.

Stay safe and let us know how we can help.

Darrion and Maggie read the e-mail, and the three thanked God for keeping their friends safe.

"I'll bet the GC up there are really ticked about them getting away," Darrion said.

The phone rang. "Bad news," Natalie said to Vicki. "They lifted your fingerprint from the radio in the car and matched it to the ones they found at the schoolhouse."

"So? They know I had their radio, but they don't know where we are."

"They're going door to door with a picture they got from the satellite broadcast. Lay low."

"What about Charlie and Bo and Ginny?"

"There's not much I can do for the

Shairtons. I haven't had any contact and I'm not sure they'll let me into the adult area."

"And Charlie?"

"I'm going to pitch an idea to a deputy commander today. Tell me about the woman you're staying with."

Vicki told her about Maggie, and Natalie gave Vicki a phone number. "This is Deputy Commander Henderson's cell number. Keep it. We might need it if my plan works. My meeting is at ten. Pray for me."

Vicki hung up and told Maggie and Darrion what she knew. Someone knocked at the door, and Maggie shooed the girls downstairs. The basement was dark except for a little light coming from the front. Vicki and Darrion quietly crept to a small window and listened as Maggie opened the door.

"May I help you?"

"Ma'am, we're looking for this girl and another one she might be traveling with," a man said.

Paper rattled and Maggie said, "Is she in some kind of trouble?"

"Just tell us if you've seen her, ma'am."

"She's awfully pretty. Kind of looks like my granddaughter in a way, but I can't help you."

"Ma'am, the gentleman down the street said two girls came to his house a couple of days ago, saying they were with some youth project and looking for people who were skeptical of the potentate's resurrection. He said he sent them over here."

"Why would he do that?" Maggie said. "You've seen the replay. There's no denying Potenate Carpathia is really alive."

"Ma'am, he said they walked over here. Did you see them or not?"

"Let me look at the picture again." Maggie didn't speak for a few moments. "I've been having trouble remembering things lately."

"It's okay, ma'am. Take your time."

"You know, now that you mention it, this girl does look like someone who stopped by here. Her hair is different in the picture, but yes, I'm sure of it."

"Could you tell us where the two might have gone?"

"No, they didn't say anything about going anywhere. Wanted to talk to me about Carpathia and, well, that's not my favorite subject. You see, the Global Community denied my insurance claim back after the—"

"I'm sorry about that, but do you know which way they went?"

"N-no, I don't . . . ," Maggie stammered and began to cry. "I don't know what's wrong with me. One minute I can think straight and the next I'm all mixed up."

"All right. If anything comes to you, would you please call me? I'd be grateful for any information."

Maggie sobbed and closed the door. Vicki watched the two officers walk away, glancing back as they reached the next house.

ELEVEN

Natalie and Charlie

Judd and Lionel spent the next few days with Westin, talking about the prophecies of the Bible and what would happen before the return of Christ at the end of the Great Tribulation. Westin asked about the adult Tribulation Force and how they were operating inside the Global Community.

After resting a day, Judd started to regain his strength. Z-Van had Westin run errands, order room service, and keep the place quiet while he was working. Westin drove Z-Van to a meeting at the palace one afternoon.

When they returned, Z-Van lingered outside Judd and Lionel's room. "You guys still believe that Bible stuff?"

"Don't you?" Lionel said. "It's all coming true."

Z-Van smiled. "You're in good company. So does Leon Fortunato."

"What?" Judd said.

"The Most High Reverend says the potentate is going to use your holy book against you."

"The most high what?" Lionel said. "I thought he was supreme commander."

"He was until His Excellency gave him the responsibility to head the new religion that will replace all others. Leon Fortunato is now the Most High Reverend Father of Carpathianism."

Judd looked away.

"The world will now have a personal deity, someone people can look to for guidance, someone they can trust, someone they know has power since he raised himself from the dead."

Westin carried papers and drawings through the hallway. Z-Van pointed to his bed. "Put them there." He turned to Judd and Lionel. "The potentate has asked that I sing at the dedication of his image in Jerusalem."

"What are you talking about?" Judd said.

"You haven't heard? Statues of the potentate are being built in major cities throughout the world. The Most High Reverend Father gave me a copy of the plans for inspiration. Each city will construct a life-size image of the potentate and display it for worship."

Judd glanced at Westin. They had talked about that very prophecy only hours before.

"The potentate hopes his resurrection will help change the minds of those who are against him. The mark he's devised is pure genius. Each one has a set of numbers that identifies where you're from. A biochip is injected under the skin so they'll know every person on the planet."

"And if we don't take the mark?" Judd said.

Z-Van smiled. "Trust me, you'll take it. I'm hoping to get mine while we're here in New Babylon. I want to do it in the city of my god, Nicolae Carpathia."

Natalie Bishop waited in the office of Deputy Commander Darryl Henderson. When he finally returned, Natalie stood, shot out her hand, and shook firmly.

Henderson was a tall man with dark, bushy eyebrows and a weird smile. He took off his glasses and rubbed at the red marks on his nose. "I see you just moved to corrections. Something wrong?"

"Sir, I'd like to help catch these kids. They're a disease to the Global Community, and I can't stand the thought of them getting away with what they've done."

Henderson sat down and leaned back in his chair. "We could use more people like you . . ." He squinted, trying to read Natalie's badge.

"Bishop, sir."

"Right. What do you want to do?"

"I've read the statements this kid Charlie has made. I think he knows more than he's letting on."

"He's not the brightest bulb, if you know what I mean." Henderson scrolled through his computer screen. "We're shipping him out to a juvenile facility Saturday."

Natalie flinched. "Let me talk with him, sir."

"You think you can do what our trained interrogators couldn't?"

"I know how these religious wackos think. I had a good look at what was in that schoolhouse. If I can convince him I'm one of them, he might lead us to them."

Henderson shook his head. "I don't know . . ."

"I'd like to talk to the man and woman from the farm too."

"Out of the question. But I will give you ten minutes with the kid."

Mark walked around the compound with the driver of the van, Colin Dial. The house had two bedrooms and was built near a mound of earth. A compact car sat in the garage and a few tools and bicycles hung on the wall.

"If I were the GC, I'd never suspect you," Mark said.

"That's the point," Colin said. "Those people at the shelter saw a big van drive away. There's no van here."

"Where's it hidden? I was too tired to notice last night."

Colin took him to the other side of the mound. Looking closely, Mark saw tracks on the grass that led to the side of the hill. At the base of the mound was a huge pile of firewood. Colin pointed a handheld device at the wood, and suddenly the pile split in two, revealing an underground bunker.

"I poured the concrete and rigged the opening myself," Colin said.

"Must have taken years."

They walked inside and Colin closed the door. "I used to be into the militia. Way before the disappearances I started digging this, storing food and supplies, and getting ready for a nuclear holocaust. I didn't want to die."

"Did you know about God?"

"I'd been to church a lot and listened to sermons, but it didn't sink in. To me the

Bible was a codebook with lots of secrets. When my wife finally showed me Tsion Ben-Judah's Web site, I knew I had missed what the Bible is all about."

Mark put the laptop next to a bank of computers that kept track of everything from the latest Global Community news to the local wildfire. "So you've turned this place into a hideout for believers?"

"Didn't plan it that way, but that's what it's become. We're real happy to have you kids and the others. Stay as long as you like."

Natalie stood outside Charlie's cell as the guard unlocked the door and left. When Charlie saw her mark, his mouth dropped open.

"My name is Natalie," she said quickly, pulling a chair to his bunk. Natalie lowered her voice. "We're just going to talk, and you're not going to say anything about seeing me before, all right?"

Charlie nodded. "I got it."

"Have they been treating you okay?"

"Yeah, the food is pretty good, and I've met a bunch of kids who need to know the truth."

"You've talked to them about God?"

"Sure. Was I not supposed to?"

Natalie smiled and leaned forward. "I'm going to get you out of here. They're sending you to a detention center this Saturday, so it has to be before then."

"What about the Shairtons?"

Natalie frowned. "They won't let me in to see them."

"Is the GC going to hurt them?"

"They're going to make everyone decide between God and Nicolae Carpathia."

"That's easy."

"Listen carefully. In order to get you out, you have to lead us to Vicki and Darrion."

Vicki and Darrion stayed out of sight in Maggie's house, watching televised coverage of the excitement over Nicolae Carpathia's return.

Dr. Neal Damosa, the head of the Global Community Department of Education, announced that the satellite schools would again hold meetings. Damosa encouraged young people to use their creativity to come up with songs, artwork, poems, and stories that celebrated the resurrection of Nicolae Carpathia. Damosa gave the address of a Web site that would soon display young people's work.

Vicki shook her head. "Next thing you know they'll have a contest for a trip to meet Carpathia in person."

Vicki asked Darrion to turn the TV off. They sat alone in Maggie's basement and talked about the other kids in the Young Trib Force and how they had been brought together.

"You really couldn't find people who are more different," Vicki said. "You and Judd come from wealthy families. I grew up in a trailer park."

"It's funny how even though we're different, our problems are pretty much the same."

Vicki nodded and ran a hand through her hair. "I keep thinking about Lionel and Judd, wondering if they'll ever get back."

Darrion smiled. "You're especially thinking of Judd, right?"

"What do you mean?"

"I could tell the first day I met you that you two had chemistry. You're going to get together. It has to happen."

Vicki blushed. She told Darrion about Judd and Nada. "I guess they were pretty serious before Nada died. I don't know how a person can rebound after something like that."

"It takes time. I'll bet when Judd gets back you'll be fighting like old times."

"I miss him so much, it's scary," Vicki said.

"I keep wondering if he'd have done something different with the schoolhouse, gotten out earlier."

Darrion put a hand on Vicki's shoulder. "It's going to be all right."

"Not for the Shairtons. If we had left the schoolhouse earlier and if I hadn't done that last satellite broadcast, the Shairtons wouldn't be behind bars."

"And if we hadn't met them, maybe Mr. Shairton wouldn't have prayed to accept Christ. Have you thought of that?"

Vicki nodded. "I just don't want anything bad to happen to them because of us."

"You've helped me see that God is in control. At first I was scared at just about everything that happened and thought it was up to us to stay alive. Now, even if the GC gets hold of us, I know that God can work something good out of anything. I'll bet the Shairtons feel the same."

Natalie tried to meet with Deputy Commander Henderson before lunch but couldn't. At two in the afternoon she finally sat in his office and told him her news.

"I had a breakthrough with that Charlie kid. He totally believes I'm one of the Judah-ites."

Henderson sat forward. "Good work. Did he tell you anything about where this Vicki girl is?"

"I guess the kids used to live near Mt. Prospect. I asked if he could take us there and he agreed if we get his dog."

"What dog?"

"From the abandoned schoolhouse. I found the thing and tried to get it to follow the kids' trail but it didn't work."

Henderson looked at his watch. "I suppose there's no harm. Let's get the dog and go."

"He doesn't want to go until tonight. He's freaked about the GC following us."

"I have an appointment tonight. Either we go now or forget it."

"He won't go in the day. Sorry. I told Charlie you were one of the Judah-ites, and he was looking forward to meeting you. I thought you wanted those girls, but maybe they're not that important."

Henderson buzzed his secretary. "Cancel my meeting tonight."

The sun was going down as Vicki took the phone from Maggie. Natalie gave exact instructions about what they were to do.

Vicki put a hand to her forehead. "Okay,

we'll be across the street. I've got the phone number and how we'll get Charlie and Phoenix, but you haven't said anything about yourself. Are you coming with us?"

"Let me play this out with the GC. I don't think they'll suspect I'm working from the inside."

"That's crazy!" Vicki said. "You know you have to get out of there before they start giving people the mark of the beast."

"Calm down. I'm a lot more valuable to you guys in here. If I can't pull it off, I'll run."

"But it might be too late."

"All my life I've wanted to do something that counted. You guys have reached so many and now I have a part in it. I want to take as many people to heaven with me as possible, so let me do this. I might even have a chance to get the Shairtons and that Zeke man out of trouble."

"I understand, but if things get hairy, promise you'll come with us."

"I promise," Natalie said.

Vicki looked at her watch and told Maggie and Darrion what to do. She sent an e-mail to the others in the Young Trib Force and asked them to pray.

TWELVE

The Rescue

VICKI sat in the driver's seat of Maggie's car across from the woman's house. Maggie and Darrion sat in the back, watching the street. For the fiftieth time, Vicki made sure Maggie's cell phone was turned on.

Darrion scooted down in her seat. "What other plan did Natalie have?"

"She was going to bring Charlie out of his cell and spray something in the guards' eyes if they got in her way," Vicki said.

"This is better," Maggie said.

Vicki and Darrion had tried to convince Maggie that she should come with the kids to Wisconsin, but the woman wouldn't listen. "I've lived here a long time, and there are a lot of people around who still need to hear the message."

"If they see your license plate, they'll find you," Vicki said.

"Took it off," Maggie said, smiling. "The rear plate is in the trunk. Put it on when you're safe."

"What are you going to do when this Henderson guy comes?" Darrion said.

"I'm going to keep him busy while you get away," Maggie said.

"You know they'll suspect you," Vicki said.

Maggie shook her head. "You really underestimate me. You think I'm just some old woman who doesn't know how to take care of herself. I've thought about it a lot.

"After you get away, they'll ask me what happened. I'll tell them how you two forced your way in and how scared I was. Then I'll make them coffee and offer some sweet rolls. They'll probably give me some kind of medal for bravery."

Vicki smiled. She hoped the GC would treat Maggie well. She looked at the cell phone again and made sure it was still on.

It was drizzling as Natalie escorted Charlie from the building in handcuffs. Deputy Commander Henderson signed Charlie out at the front desk. The clerk at the front questioned Henderson. Natalie thought about jumping in the GC vehicle and taking off, but the man cleared up the problem and followed as she got Charlie in the backseat. Natalie climbed in next to Charlie and fought off Phoenix as he licked his friend's face. Charlie laughed, awkwardly trying to pet Phoenix.

Natalie leaned toward the man and whispered, "It might be good if we took his cuffs off. You know, a show of faith."

Henderson winked and handed her the keys. "Charlie, we're going to get you out of those so you can pet your dog."

"I sure appreciate it, sir," Charlie said. "I had no idea I'd meet two followers of Dr. Ben-Judah here. How did you find out about him?"

Henderson smiled as he drove toward Mt. Prospect. "Oh, you know, I saw his Web site, read his message, and pretty soon I was just praying away."

"Has it changed your life like it has mine?" Charlie said.

"Oh yes, definitely. I'm a much better person now that I believe . . . uh, what you believe. God is so much more real to me now."

Henderson turned right on Mt. Prospect Road. It was fine in places, torn up in others, so the man slowed. A few of the streetlights worked. Others were broken or had burned out long ago.

"Did the kids meet in a house or some other kind of building?" Henderson asked Charlie.

"It was sort of a house, but they used it like an apartment building. I think I'll know it when I see it."

"Natalie says you don't remember the street?"

"Didn't you say it started with a C?" Natalie said.

Henderson glared at her. "Let him talk, Bishop."

"Yeah, I think it started with a C," Charlie said.

"Central?"

"Yeah, that's it."

Henderson found Central and drove a few blocks. Natalie placed her hand inside her coat, found her cell phone, and secretly punched the number Vicki had given her. She gave it time to ring and hung up.

"Anything look familiar?" Henderson said, slowing at an abandoned business and two burned-out cars.

"Nothing yet, sir."

Henderson pulled to the side and stopped. Charlie's eyes darted and Phoenix whimpered.

"Tell me the truth," Henderson finally said.

Natalie sat forward. "Sir, I told you—"

"I'm not talking to you. I'm talking to him." Henderson grabbed Charlie's arm and pulled him forward. "You don't know where those two are any more than I do."

Charlie looked wildly at Natalie and back at the man.

"You told me you knew where their hideout was," Natalie said.

"You're supposed to be my friends," Charlie said. "I don't understand."

Henderson threw the car in gear and turned around. He tossed the handcuffs into the backseat. "Cuff him. We're taking him home."

Natalie couldn't believe Vicki hadn't phoned. Was it possible Natalie's signal hadn't gone through? She pulled Charlie's arms behind his back and clicked the cuffs but didn't put them on. "Just keep your arms behind you," she whispered.

Natalie pulled out her cell phone. "I don't believe this. I'm calling headquarters and telling them we're coming back in."

She dialed Vicki's number and made sure it rang. She ended the call and threw the phone onto the floor. "I hate this thing. I can never get through."

"Don't bother," Henderson said. "They don't need to know we're coming back."

"Sir, I'm sorry. I thought for sure he was legit."

Henderson shook his head. "I should have known better than to trust—"

Before he could finish his sentence, Henderson's phone rang. He wrestled with his coat and pulled it from his pocket. "Yeah."

Henderson held the phone away from his ear. Natalie leaned forward and listened.

"Is this Mr. Henderson?" an older woman said.

"Who is this?"

"I just called your office and they gave me this number."

"Well, they shouldn't have. If you have business with the Morale Monitors, call me there in the morning."

"But—"

Natalie's heart sank as Henderson hung up. "Who was that?"

"Some old bat."

The phone rang again. Natalie was afraid he was going to turn his phone off. Instead, he answered it and cursed.

"You watch your language, young man," the woman said. "I called to give you information on those two girls you're looking for, but if you're going to treat me like that, I'll just hang up."

"No, no! I'm sorry. I've had trouble with people in the office giving out this number." He pulled to the side of the road and stopped. "Please, what two girls are you talking about?"

"The two they were looking for the other day. Teenagers. Young, pretty little things. I had a hard time believing they were the ones you wanted until I tried to get them to leave."

Henderson pulled out a pen. "Okay. Give me your exact location."

The woman rattled off a street address near the GC station. "I'm using my cell phone so they won't hear me. I'm telling them I'm ordering a pizza, so ring the bell—"

"No!" Henderson shouted. "Don't tell them anything. Just leave the front door open and I'll come in."

"I'll try, but they notice everything."

"I'll find a way inside. Just keep them there. I'm about fifteen minutes away."

"I'll do my best."

Henderson hung up and raced down the road. Charlie tried to keep his hands behind him as they bounced.

"What's happening?" Natalie said.

Henderson scowled. "Your friend back there wasn't even close. We're going to nab those two girls tonight."

Vicki took the cell phone from Maggie, and the woman got out of the car. Vicki and Darrion got out and hugged Maggie. "We don't know how we'll ever be able to thank you," Vicki said.

Maggie smiled. "You just keep telling people the truth about God. That's payment enough for me."

The three stood in the drizzling rain until Maggie told Vicki and Darrion to get into the car. "You two are going to catch your death of cold before we get that boy back."

"What about the car?" Vicki said.

"It's yours. You and your friends use it however you see fit."

Maggie went back into her house. Rain poured, pelting the windshield. Vicki watched the drops trail down the glass.

Finally, a car turned onto the street and turned off its lights. As it slowly approached, Vicki and Darrion scooted toward the floor and waited.

Natalie took a deep breath as they approached Maggie's house. She knew the next few moments might mean the difference between freedom and a GC prison for the kids.

She had hoped Henderson wouldn't call for backup. She knew he had an ego and wanted to make the arrest himself. As he slipped the car into park, he dialed his cell phone and asked to speak to an officer on duty.

"I thought you were one of us," Charlie said. "You don't believe in God?"

Henderson turned with a smirk. "I got news for you, pal. The only god I believe in rose from the dead last weekend. You'd better get used to following his orders."

The rain came harder, drops banging onto the roof. Natalie glanced to her left and noticed an older car parked opposite Maggie's house. She nudged Charlie.

Henderson gave the address and asked for a squad car to back him up. The officer said it would take another five minutes for someone to get there, and Henderson hung up. "I'm not going to wait any longer."

Natalie opened her door. "I'm going with you."

"No way. You stay with him and watch the front."

"I didn't sign up to do baby-sitting," Natalie spat.

Henderson paused. "I gave you a direct

order. Stay here and make sure they don't come out the front."

"What if they do?"

"Get out and use your Mace to subdue them."

Henderson closed the door quietly and crept up the sidewalk. Charlie started to speak, but Natalie put a finger to her lips. She glanced at the car across the street and saw some movement on the driver's side.

Henderson looked in a window at the front of the house, then rounded some bushes and tried to see in another.

"Come on, Henderson," Natalie whispered to herself, "go to the back before those other GC goons get here."

Phoenix jumped into the front seat and Charlie grabbed him. "Hold on to him," Natalie said.

Henderson tried to get in the backyard but couldn't. He circled the front yard again, glancing at the car as he passed. The front door opened and an old woman waved Henderson inside. "That must be Maggie," Natalie said. "But what's she doing?"

Henderson ran into the house and Maggie waved excitedly. Natalie threw open the squad-car door and yelled at Charlie. He came bounding out with Phoenix in his arms.

Vicki started Maggie's car and Darrion opened the back door. When Phoenix saw Vicki he yelped. Charlie jumped in after him.

"Get in!" Vicki yelled at Natalie.

"No," Natalie said, her hair soaked from the rain. "I can handle this. Just get out of here before . . ."

Vicki glanced in the rearview mirror and saw two headlights and flashing lights approaching. Maggie's front door opened with a crash, and Henderson shouted from the top of the stairs.

"Hurry!" Natalie said as she slammed the back door.

Judd awoke with a start early in the morning in New Babylon. He walked through the massive hotel rooms, but no one stirred. Z-Van had worked late into the night and still snored. Lionel, Westin, and the others slept soundly.

Judd went back to bed and lay there. He thought of Z-Van's trip to Jerusalem and what would happen there. Judd felt like he was being drawn back to Israel . . . but why? He pushed the thought from his mind and

suddenly had the impression that someone
was in trouble.

Judd knelt by his bed and asked God to
protect his friends. He prayed first for Vicki.

ABOUT THE AUTHORS

Jerry B. Jenkins (www.jerryjenkins.com) is the writer of the Left Behind series. He owns the Jerry B. Jenkins Christian Writers Guild, an organization dedicated to mentoring aspiring authors. Former vice president for publishing for the Moody Bible Institute of Chicago, he also served many years as editor of *Moody* magazine and is now Moody's writer-at-large.

His writing has appeared in publications as varied as *Reader's Digest*, *Parade*, *Guideposts*, in-flight magazines, and dozens of other periodicals. Jenkins's biographies include books with Billy Graham, Hank Aaron, Bill Gaither, Luis Palau, Walter Payton, Orel Hershiser, and Nolan Ryan, among many others. His books appear regularly on the *New York Times*, *USA Today*, *Wall Street Journal*, and *Publishers Weekly* bestseller lists.

Jerry is also the writer of the nationally syndicated sports story comic strip *Gil Thorp*, distributed to newspapers across the United States by Tribune Media Services.

Jerry and his wife, Dianna, live in Colorado and have three grown sons.

Dr. Tim LaHaye (www.timlahaye.com), who conceived the idea of fictionalizing an account of the Rapture and the Tribulation, is a noted author, minister, and nationally recognized speaker on Bible prophecy. He is the founder of both Tim LaHaye Ministries and The PreTrib Research Center. He also recently cofounded the Tim LaHaye School of Prophecy at Liberty University. Presently Dr. LaHaye speaks at many of the major Bible prophecy conferences in the U.S. and Canada, where his current prophecy books are very popular.

Dr. LaHaye holds a doctor of ministry degree from Western Theological Seminary and a doctor of literature degree from Liberty University. For twenty-five years he pastored one of the nation's outstanding churches in San Diego, which grew to three locations. It was during that time that he founded two accredited Christian high schools, a Christian school system of ten schools, and Christian Heritage College.

Dr. LaHaye has written over forty books that have been published in more than thirty languages. He has written books on a wide variety of subjects, such as family life, temperaments, and Bible prophecy. His current fiction works, the Left Behind series, written with Jerry B. Jenkins, continue to appear on the best-seller lists of the Christian Booksellers Association, *Publishers Weekly*, *Wall Street Journal*, *USA Today*, and the *New York Times*.

He is the father of four grown children and grandfather of nine. Snow skiing, waterskiing, motorcycling, golfing, vacationing with family, and jogging are among his leisure activities.

The Future Is Clear

Check out the exciting Left Behind: The Kids series

BOOKS #29 AND #30 COMING SOON!

Discover the latest about the Left Behind series and complete line of products at

www.leftbehind.com

Hooked on the exciting
Left Behind: The Kids series?
Then you'll love the dramatic audios!

Listen as the characters come to life in this theatrical
audio that makes the saga of those left behind
even more exciting.

High-tech sound effects, original music,
and professional actors will have you
on the edge of your seat.

Experience the heart-stopping action and
suspense of the end times for yourself!

Three exciting volumes available on CD or cassette.